desperados

Rafael Joseph Zepeda

First Edition
ISBN # 978-0615734583

Edited by Sierra Patheal

Layout: Chan Plett
Cover Design: John Pierce
Cover Photo: R. Taylor Zepeda

Press and Press Contact Information:
World Parade Books
5267 Warner Avenue #191
Huntington Beach, CA 92649
worldparadebooks@gmail.com
www.worldparadebooks.com

For John Pierce, Pat Webster, and Sam Wilson

For Tim Grobaty

Hugo Zepeda

"In the wildness is the preservation of the world."
Henry David Thoreau

1

To begin with, there is the sad tale of my right foot. One day, I asked my wife Jean to see my grandfather's clerk's Colt .45, which I'd given her a year before to keep the bandits at bay while I was out at sea. She said that she remembered it was in the closet, up on the top shelf, somewhere. She stood on a chair and moved a suitcase to the right and reached in to feel around in the dark. I stood there, looking up. She often put things in exotic cubby holes without telling anyone where they were.

"You sure it's up there?" I asked her. "Why would you put it somewhere where you couldn't get it?"

"Don't start griping," she said. "I don't like guns."

Then I heard two bumps and then a bang. Those sounds had come from my Sicilian grandfather's Colt revolver, falling from the shelf and hitting the chair she stood on and then the floor. It was the short-barreled version of "The Gun that Won the West," at least part of the West. The pistol had been involved in a lot of troubles that both my Sicilian grandfather and my father after him seemed good at getting into.

Standing there and looking up at Jean, I felt the bullet slam like a mallet into my right foot. I fell to the floor and started moaning from the pain.

"What happened?" Jean said.

"I've been shot," I said. "You shot me."

"What in the hell are you doing standing there, anyway?" she said.

"Why'd you drop the damn thing?" I said.

"It's oily," she said. "I didn't try to shoot you. Anyway, I didn't know that the stupid thing was loaded."

"Why would I give you an unloaded gun for protection

from burglars?" I said.

"Just take me to the hospital, for Christ's sake. Get me a towel or something."

At the time, we were at home in Playa Grande, which is a little beach town in Orange County, where there are few violent crimes and where the cops are legendary for bopping many young people's heads with night sticks on Saint Patrick's Day and giving traffic and parking tickets galore. I have always recommended to my friends that they don't drive through there at all if they can avoid it, especially if they've had a couple of beers. The cops give more DUIs per capita than any other town in California. I know a lot about the way they operate. I'd been a cop there for a year and a half, but I quit because I couldn't stand the bad vibes that were transmitted from friends and relatives when they wanted to smoke a joint or let their dog run on the beach, or break any other stupid law for doing something harmless, which I, of course, as a cop, was supposed to bust people for. I should have realized all of this before I applied for the job, but I'd just thought about the wonderful pension and the early retirement with which I would one day in the future disappear into Baja, or Idaho, forever and ever, to fish and watch the birds fly by.

Anyway, the bullet shattered a few of my phalanxes as it put a tunnel through my right foot, then went into the hardwood floor. The x-ray of my foot looked like a map of the constellations surrounded by little dog biscuits. That is how I was then declared disabled and therefore retired from my position for twenty-two years, on and off, as first mate on tugs, faithfully serving the Sabatasso Brothers Tugboat Company. That stretch of time had only been interrupted by my one-and-a-half-year stint as a cop, a very shitty job, as I said, for a guy like me. I had been bad at banging heads on St. Patrick's Day, a day of much festivity in our quaint town, since there are four Irish bars and a couple of other bars that also become Irish bars for the day on Main Street, all of which serve green beer and give out green cellophane leprechaun hats to everyone who attends "Finnegan's Wake." A three-foot dummy of Finnegan, shamrocks emblazoned on his clothes and bowler hat and a pipe in his mouth, lies in state in a black wooden coffin that travels from bar to bar, up and down the street, so that all of the bars' clients can then pay homage to Finnegan, James Joyce, Samuel Beckett, William Butler Yeats, and the rest of those Irish writers. That accident with Jean and the pistol was what had started my family's grand ideas brewing about my taking over the flower shop and working there, even though I wanted no part of it. My father and mother always said, "Someone has to take it over when we retire."

Then later on, when my father had made his predictable departure, I was the obvious selection, the chosen one, to take over the joint, since I "wasn't working anymore," they figured. My brother Art was happy to see me take it over, since he wanted no part of it either. That is, except for the money part of the deal, which always seems to be a consideration. But, to tell the truth, aside from all my protesting about coming back and becoming the florist of the day once again, I had been hitting the tequila pretty hard down at Cinco Casas, a couple of hundred miles down the coast from T. J. So the family was, Art said, "very concerned about" my "mental health and tequila intake." My foot had taken three months to heal enough to go without a cane, while I had sat at home, my foot up and a bottle of beer on the table beside me. That was when Jean told me to get out of her life.

She had said, "I wish that old cowboy gun had shot you in the head instead of the foot."

Then I had packed up and driven south into Baja and holed up in my old Airstream down on the coast, just surf fishing and paddling the old log out for some negotiable waves once in a while, unmolested by wife and family. I dug clams a couple of times a week since they made such a wonderful chowder, surf fished, and dove for lobsters or scraped abalone off the rocks for breakfast, lunch, and dinner. And I rode my old Gordie log once in a while. I'd gone south to recuperate and to mend my shattered foot and my shit-filled head. At Cinco Casas, I was getting to be a tanned and healthy son of a bitch, even though I'd usually put away a fifth of tequila or so every couple of days.

My Old Rusty Horseshoe, commonly called Herradura, went down smooth as a milk shake, and many of the other respected brands were just plain hard to turn down. When some mota came my way, I'd smoke that too, always being careful not to smoke after drinking, just smoking and then drinking. Everyone down in the little colony of Cinco Casas knew that I had once been a cop, so, even if it had only been for a year and a half, they treated me as if I was a retired general.

That day back in October, my brother Art had driven up in his old Cherokee, one Tuesday, or Wednesday, or Sunday. I sat outside in a cowhide-covered chair under my palm palapa, my stout Mexican water glass, a fifth of Herradura, and a cool bottle of Pacifico on the table in front of me, and I'd watched him walk up the hill past my field of tequila bottles. He carried a manila envelope under his arm, and he walked like all of the Sicilians on my mother's side, as if he had a cracker on his butt that he didn't want to break. It was probably a gene handed down from some Phoenician or Viking who had dragged his oar through Sicilian waters a thousand years ago, or so.

"Come in out of the sun, stranger," I said.

"I just came down for a little talk," he said and smiled, then sat beside me.

I went in the trailer and got him a Pacifico, then came out and sat down, opened his beer, and handed it to him. He and I are close in age, he being just three years younger, and we get along just fine most of the time. We have seen a few miles of rocky roads together, with my father being such a nutcase. Art was still pissed off at me for trying to shoot that apple off of his head when I was nine and Art six with a bamboo plant stake I'd notched like an arrow. Even so, we had always been friends as well as brothers. He still had the small, round scar like an eclipse

8

of the moon between his eyes. At nine years old, for a short time, I'd thought I was William Tell.

Art took a drink of his beer. "You've been down here a long time," he said. "Everybody's worried about you."

"I'm just fine," I said. "I'm taking the cure from modern society."

"Even Jean's worried about you," he said. "She thought you'd come back after you cooled down for a month or so. But you never showed up."

As I said, Jean had kicked me out of the house for being "a complainer and a jerk," she said, even though she had been the one to shoot me and cause me to be laid up at the house in the first place. To tell the truth, as I recall, I never complained out loud. I just must have looked as if I was a complainer.

"She's getting the checks every month, isn't she?" I said.

"Yeah, but she's worried," Art said. "She thinks that you might be dead down here somewhere. People aren't supposed to disappear for six months without a word to anyone, even if they have been banished by their wives. I guess they don't have calendars around here, for Christ's sake," he said. "First you come down here and get lost, then Pop takes off for who-knows-where, Mexico, too. I just don't see the attraction."

"Tranquility," I said. "The distant past."

I didn't even try to explain my tequila calendar to Art, since I knew he'd think I was even more nuts than he already thought I was.

"Where'd Pop go this time?" I asked.

"He's roaming around Mexico someplace, looking for trouble," he said. "He's been gone for a month. These are a bunch of very weird postcards and letters that he sent." He pushed the manila envelope toward me.

Down the hill and out to sea, a large flock of pelicans cruised the trough of the swell of a wave. They rode the updraft of the swells rolling in and skimmed the water as they flew south. I counted them, as usual.

"Fifty-three," I said. "Today's record."

We watched them as they glided by without effort on the updraft.

"A lot can happen in six months," he said. "Pop takes off for parts unknown. Mom gets all worried and stressed and pissed off. She's had the flu, or depression, or something, for weeks, so the shop is closed, and no money's coming in."

"Why didn't someone tell me Pop was gone?" I said.

"You're down here in Baja, remember? Where's your telephone?" he said. "Where's your damn mailbox? You're out of touch, man."

"No doubt Mom's doing the Sicilian martyr routine," I said.

"You called it," he said.

We both laughed and drank more beer. Our mother had always gone into a dark place and had a dark expression on her face when bad things happened. She had always been worried about where we were, worried about us becoming Mafiosos, worried about The Evil Eye, worried about everything. As if being half-Sicilian made you want to be a crook. Not that we hadn't thought about life as a banditos.

Anyway, the problem now was our old man. He had a way of taking off like Wily Coyote for a while every few years, when he got off his medication, and he was a full-blooded Mexican, or a full blooded mestizo, if those things are possible, so he usually headed south into his Old Country. But before, he had always come back in a week or so.

"And everybody's wondering what's going to happen," he said.

"Wondering what about what's going to happen?" I said.

"If anyone's going to take the shop over," he said. "Mom's too distraught and sick to do anything."

"So who's elected?" I said.

"Not me," he said. "I have a job."

"Same here," I said. "This is my job--retired seaman, ex-

10

cop, old surfer, patient fisherman, clam digger, pelican counter, and tequila connoisseur."

"Somebody has to take it over, one of these days," Art said.

"Why?" I said.

"Because it's a money making business, I guess," he said.

"That's the only thing good about it," I said.

"You know how to run it," he said, "and you have to do something until we figure out how you can get Pop and bring him home and get him on some medication."

"So now I'm supposed to take over the shop until we know where Pop went," I said, "and then go and get Pop, too? . . . I told you, I am doing something, right now and right here."

He looked over at my field of tequila bottles. Beyond the trailer to the south they were in rows, each row seven across and twenty-four deep. One hundred and sixty-eight days. They were mostly Herradura bottles, a few Conmemorativos, a few Tres Mujeres, and even a few Patrons, from when some of my affluent friends had dropped by. Each of my months had twenty-eight days. That way, every three months I had a six-day Leap Week. I had never figured out that thing with the knuckles, nor could I seem to remember the rhyme, so I had made my own calendar out of tequila bottles, some found on the beach, but mostly those drained by me and various friends. Screw the news, screw birthdays, screw untimely deaths, screw chubascos and earthquakes, especially during Leap Week. Screw everything else, and all the rest, too, during the rest of the weeks. The tequila bottles were beautiful as they glistened and shone in the afternoon sun. I knew exactly how long I had been gone according to my tequila bottles, theoretically, anyway. It wasn't the exact and precise Aztec calendar of old, but it was all mine. I knew how long I had been there, metaphorically speaking.

"What's with the empty bottles?" he said. "It looks like someone's been drinking a little tequila around here."

"A lot of people down here drink a little tequila," I said. "It's a tradition. Anyway, all those bottles aren't mine. They're just my way of counting the days."

"You can't just keep sitting here, getting fucked up and being a beachcomber," he said.

"Oh yes I can," I said.

"Don't you want to see your kids?" he said. "Don't you want to rescue the old man from getting killed by the banditos or thrown in jail for being wacko, wherever he is?"

"My kids are all grown up," I said. "And the old man will probably come back one day soon, soon as he isn't flying so damn high. He always has, and besides, he has too many of his cars parked at his house to stay gone for long. He loves them like they're his children. Like they're alive, like real horses. Anyway, if someone wants to see me, they all know where I am. You're here, aren't you?"

"It wasn't just Grandpa's Colt that shot you," he said. "You're psychologically wounded."

"Of course I am," I said. "Just like everybody else is . . . So let's see these cards and letters in the Mystery Envelope."

"Like I said, they're just some weird postcards and letters from the old man," he said, "like the ones I was talking about. Crazy ones, of course. I thought you might like to see a few places he's been."

He opened the clip on the envelope and dumped the pile of postcards and letters out on the table, and I picked through them. There were cards from Mulage, La Paz, Loretto, a few from the mainland--Mazatlan, San Blas, Puerto Vallarta, Jojutlan. The card on top was postmarked from Mulege. It had a picture of a girl's naked back, just her bikini bottom on, and she was wearing a gold sombrero. The back of the card read:

Hola Todos,
]Don't worry about me. I'm fantastico and pretty sober, too.
Amor, pesetas, y tempo para gustarlo,
Sabas Joaquín Murrieta Gauguin Catalpa,
AKA your Pop

12

Every once in a while, when on a manic high, Pop liked to think that he might be the reincarnated Joaquin Murrieta, the infamous California bandit, or at least, he always seemed to wish he was. Joaquin Murrieta had been one of his heroes since he was a little kid, so it was his running joke to call himself by the bandito's name. And as for Paul Gauguin, he loved his life, that he had left town to paint and enjoy the wahines. Of course, he never cared for the syphilis part of the story. The card was from a couple of weeks back. Art said that the old man had taken off for Mexico with a pocket full of cash, his black Stetson on his head. He had chosen his four-wheel drive Ram Charger from the five cars he owned that were parked on the street and in his backyard. The cards and letters had stopped a week ago, so there was no telling where he had gone since then.

"Maybe if I stay here, he'll just drive up for a visit," I said.

"Not likely," Art said. "He's way down south somewhere, screwing around. You have to go get him or he'll end up in jail or dead, the way he's acting now."

"First off, you have to know about where someone is if you want to find him," I said.

2

The flower business smells, just like my old man always says. The delivery van waited at the curb beside the shop, my cousin Lawrence pacing back and forth with a Kool butt stuck between his hairy neo-hipster lips. I finished sticking the leather fern in a casket spray--seventy-five bucks, plus tax--of white stock streamers, red carnations, and ribbon reading "Beloved Husband & Father" in gold stick-on letters. I'd been biding my time, waiting for some current message that would give me a direction in which to go.

The casket spray was for a man named David McMullen, age 79, who'd died from cardiac arrest and then the onset of pneumonia, the old-people mercy killer. His wife and son had come two days before. She had worn a dark blue dress and a powder blue scarf, and she had a face like a cherub framed by hair that was dyed blue-gray. David Jr. had gray, coffee-stained teeth and hepatic breath, and he was the king of assholes. They stood at the counter, David Jr. with a frozen leer on his face, she with a bewildered expression saying she had been wounded by her son's sarcastic jabs a few times before.

Pointing at the photo of the spray, I said, "We put two dozen red carnations in the middle, and these are white stock. This is the seventy-five dollar casket spray."

"Anything that isn't too expensive, or too dead--that's what we want," David Jr. said and smiled.

His mother looked over at him, as if expecting him to be a pain in the ass, then looked up at me and said, "That sounds very nice. He liked red and white."

Then she wrote the check for the price, plus tax for the governor.

"Hey," McMullen junior said, "you know why we came to this place?" He looked at me and smiled an all-knowing-asshole smile.

"No," I said, "why?"

"I was down in Loreto fishing a few days ago," he said, "and this old guy wearing a cowboy hat is at the bar. He's speaking Mexican, but he's got these blue eyes, so I don't know what he is. Maybe a half-breed. He's having a good time's all I know. He's buying tequila for everyone, even the Mexicans, so I got to talking to him and told him I was from around Playa Grande, and he says, 'If you're ever in need of beautiful flowers, look this shop up.' He hands me a card, and he says, 'You never can tell when you'll need them. Weddings, births, funerals. Flowers for all occasions. Death's waiting at the curb, you know,' he said. Then he laughs and slaps me on the back and orders another round of tequila. 'You stab him, we slab him,' he says."

"When was this?" I asked.

"Three days ago, like I said." He picked his nose with his little finger.

"Did he say where he was going?" I asked.

"No. He just handed me this." David Jr. pulled out his wallet and from it a business card. "'Catalpa Flowers, The Rite Spot,'" he read. "'Sabas and Mary Catalpa, proprietors.'" He handed me the card. It was one of the cards from the shop, all right. It smelled of fish, probably a Tutuava, nearly extinct, caught illegally by David Jr.

Jesus, I thought, there's no telling from whence news appears, this coming from the king of pendejos. So he's still down in Baja, I thought. Maybe I can find him down there.

Finally, the McMullens left, and I was left there, wondering what to do first.

Two days later, I was finishing the casket spray for Mr. McMullen, red and white, as requested. I carried the spray out

15

to the van and put it on a wooden lettuce crate in the back.

"Shit, man," my pseudo-hipster cousin, Larry the Slob, said, "they're gonna shit at Stetler's." He looked as his watch. By the clock on the wall, it was 6:15, and the rosary was to be at seven.

"You'll make it," I said. "And Mr. McMullen will never know the difference, I promise." I slammed the doors closed. Larry dropped his smoking Kool in the gutter and stuck another between his lips. He hopped in the van and sped off north, toward Stetler's Mortuary.

My wounded right foot ached from standing in stock stems and dead flowers all day, and my head ached from the recently-received weird news about my father, so I limped back into the shop. The shop wasn't much of a showplace, just a shack on a corner with plate glass windows in the front and a tin roof, but it smelled good, of wet earth and combinations of flower odors, like a greenhouse. In the summer it was a sweathouse and in the winter a freezer locker. It had been my father and mother's place since Pop had decided to go into business on his own when he was twenty-four. He'd been working for Ben and Carrie Vasso, Sephardic Jews who had a place seven blocks up Pacific Avenue, north of Pacific Coast Highway. He'd learned a lot from them. They'd treated him like a son, even though they had two sons of their own. They hadn't even gotten that mad at him for starting up a business just seven blocks down the street. They'd sent him a grand opening arrangement, a ribbon with "Good Luck in your New Adventure," when you'd think they would have sent an arsonist.

I sat down at the desk and lit a little Schimmelpenninck cigar, then took my right shoe off and rubbed my foot. I had things to think about, my old man, Baja California, Mexico in general, and my god damned foot. I nodded to myself and kept my mouth shut, since I knew what Art had said was true. I was the one who had to go and get him. David McMullen Jr. had made the first real sighting of Pop in the six weeks he'd been gone. I looked out the open glass door, past the azalea and mum plants and the philodendrons, as I rubbed my foot, and thought it looked as if the time had come to leave the shop in other hands, or in no hands at all for a while, and head south of the border to find Pop, to make sure that he didn't get thrown in jail, or robbed, or killed, since he was wacko once again. I had to try to bring him home, which was definitely going to be a trying task.

3

A week before my son Pete and I took off south, I got a phone call from Brian Martinet, an old friend. Brian was doing very well with a few restaurants that he owned and with his investments in the stock market. He'd always been better than most people with money. I'd known him since we'd gone to catechism classes with the nuns when we were seven years old. I was sitting in my apartment near the beach, where I'd gone after Jean had kicked me out. I'd kept it while I'd been at Cinco Casas, since having the trailer there in Baja didn't cost much. Anyway, I had planned to come north again, some day in my distant future.

"Did you give my number to Cindy?" Brian said.

"Who? I didn't give your number to anyone."

"She called me last night," he said.

"Why in the hell would I give anyone your number, Brian?" I said.

"You told Gil, and he called me and tried to sell me life insurance. Did you tell Cindy about me?" he said.

"Cindy who?" I said.

"Cindy Paquette," he said. "She called me up and said that she wanted to talk to me about 'something important.' Did you talk to her?"

"No. Should I have talked to her? What was so important?" I said.

Cindy Paquette was a girl we had both known in high school, our Homecoming Queen.

"I asked her, but she just said, 'It's secret,' so she couldn't talk about it on the phone. Did you tell her that I was in

Laguna?"

"No. Man, I haven't seen her in a million years. I just got back from being in Baja for six months," I said. "What are you talking about?"

"When you told Gil Preston about me last year," he said, "that son of a bitch called me up and tried to sell me life insurance."

Gil Preston was a redheaded guy who we'd both also gone to catechism classes with, from the time when we all were seven until we were twelve and were confirmed. He had always been a guy who carried trouble with him like a Saint Christopher's medal.

"Take it easy, man," I said. "I told Gil that you were doing well, making some money. So what? It's the truth."

"But he called me, just because you told him," Brian said.

"No," I said, "he called you, just because he's an asshole, and just because your goddamn number is in the phonebook. Anyway, I have other problems. I'm getting ready to go to Mexico and find my wayward father."

"Oh, too bad," Brian said. "Look, do me a favor. Just tell everyone you see from the old days that I'm in Hawaii."

"Sure thing, Brian," I said. "Maybe I'll see you when I get back."

As I said, Brian had always been good with money, but he'd also always had a way of being paranoid. Intelligent people seem to often be that way. Too much imagination, I suppose.

Our Homecoming Queen in high school, Cindy Paquette, was a pretty girl, even though she had never been a brainchild. To tell you the truth, I always thought she looked a lot like a chicken because of the way her neck and chin went together and the way her blonde hair swept up in back with that short hairdo of hers. She was what we called a socialite in those days, but of course that was a million years ago, when the Hippies hadn't even been named yet. I remember seeing her at the prom dance at the end of our senior year, as she stood there on the stage holding pink roses in her arms as if the bouquet was a baby that she was afraid to drop. My folks had sent those roses over that afternoon, my mother making sure Pop hadn't shoved a few old ones in there. She wanted to be sure the roses wouldn't be dead by the time Cindy got on stage at the formal dance. My mother had even stuck the stems of the roses into plastic tubes, the stems cut on an angle, so that they would draw water.

Cindy wore a pink formal with pink spaghetti straps, her sloping shoulders and pink skin almost the color of the dress and its lace. It billowed out at the bottom like The Liberty Bell, and you could just see her pink satin shoes sticking out beneath the hem. Beside her stood Dan Geffen, an acquaintance of mine and football player of slight renown who looked a little bit like the young Superman without the cape whose father owned a hospital in town and a clinic down in San Diego. He wore a black tuxedo and a pink shirt and bow tie to match Cindy's dress. His dark hair was short, parted like Peter Gunn's, and he had wide shoulders and a six-foot frame that looked good in a tux, chiseled features, and a smile that looked as if he owned the world, which was almost true. The perfect specimen, headed for USC.

They both stood there on the stage like those little plastic statues on a wedding cake. She smiled as the band played our school song, but even then, she looked a little bewildered at it all. He smiled down at her, and then the band started to play "Come Go With Me," that song by the Del Vikings, and our King and Queen walked out onto the dance floor, and Dan took her in his arms and crushed the pink roses between them as they began to dance that slow waltz that they'd both learned at Cotillions in the seventh grade, except they held their hands a little lower, and their bodies were much closer together. The spotlight followed them across the dance floor, there in the Las Flores Hotel ballroom. We all watched them and applauded politely. Then other couples started to stroll out onto the dance floor and the lights dimmed, and I grabbed my future wife Jean

Costello's hand and we joined everyone in a slow cruiser dance, my half-pint of Bacardi rum in Jean's black satin purse.

Late that night, a dozen of us ended up at Dan Geffen's house, in the rumpus room, with Ray Charles playing on the stereo, me on the couch with Jean, the others on couches throughout the house, and Dan Geffen pawing and feeling up Cindy on the glider that sat beside his kidney-shaped pool outside.

That had been the last time that I'd seen Cindy Paquette, twenty-two years earlier, but I'd heard she had married a guy named Vince McKelvey, someone whose name and face I knew, but little more. I'd heard some time ago that he had become a fireman for the county.

Then, a week before heading south after Pop, I was at my apartment, half a block from the beach, and one morning a couple of days later, I'd gotten on my bike to ride down to the pier and look at the waves. In front of the house next door, an old, brown, dirty Thunderbird was parked, a woman wearing big, dark glasses behind the wheel. The palm tree above the car was full of crows, and some bird shit had come down onto the windshield, right in the woman's view, along with some other bird shit she'd collected elsewhere. I pedaled by the car, toward the beach, and looked over at the woman as I passed, and for some reason I knew that it was Cindy Paquette, even though her hair wasn't blonde anymore, and she had large shades on, and it had been twenty-two years since I'd seen her. I circled and pedaled back toward the car and stopped beside the driver's side, then looked in, and she looked over at me.

"Hey Cindy," I said. "That's you, isn't it?"

"Oh, hi, Sabas," she said.

"What's going on?" I said, smiling at her.

"Oh, I'm just looking for a Lyons Van and Storage," she said.

"Oh," I said, "a Lyons Van and Storage. I don't think there's one of those around here anymore."

21

"Yes there is," she said, taking off her dark glasses and staring at me. When I looked into her blue eyes, it was like looking at the sea in the Caribbean. Her pupils were dilated and her eyelids half-closed. "I know that it's around here somewhere."

As far as I remembered, Lyons Van and Storage had gone out of business at least twenty years ago, but I humored her. It wasn't any of my business if she thought that Lyons Van and Storage was still around.

"Maybe you need to look in the phonebook," I said. "I have one in the house."

"No, no, no, I looked in there. That's okay," she said, as she fidgeted with her purse on her lap. "I didn't know you lived around here."

Sure you didn't, I thought. "For a couple years," I said. "So how have you been?"

I realized then that she had somehow found out where I lived, probably so she could get to Brian Martinet. I wondered where Vince McKelvey had been during all of this.

"I'm okay," she said.

"And what have you been doing?"

"Oh," she said, "I was over seeing my kids, trying to see them, and the cigarette fell down on my pants and I started hitting it and then my pants were on fire and my kids were inside the house and Vince was in the house, you know Vince but he's a mean asshole, and he was looking out and he wouldn't let the kids out because he was fucking that babysitter and the fire started going and going and the fire department came because he's on the fire department I guess but my pants were on fire and the seat and everything was burning and they got me out and put powder and water on me and Vince was in the window watching me with my girls' faces there and that babysitter Tamara bitch that he's fucking and he was looking out and I just want to see them but he's on the fire department and they keep spraying that white stuff all over me and so I'm waiting for . . ."

All the while she kept rummaging in her purse, and then

22

she stared out the window, through the bird shit, toward something that I couldn't see, something out there in Weirdville.

"So I'd better find Lyons Van and Storage."

"Are you going to be all right?" I said.

"I want to talk to Brian Martinet," she said. "He won't talk to me, but I think he can help me get my kids back, because he used to help me all the time in school, because he was smart in geometry and other stuff."

She started the car, and a big cloud of smoke rose up and blew inland as it loped along on what sounded like six of its eight cylinders.

"Well, nice talking to you, Cindy," I said. "Take it easy."

"Yes, I got to go to Lyons Van and Storage," she said, "to get some boxes and stuff, so that I can move."

She started inching the car along as I stood there.

"Goodbye," I said. "Be careful out there."

"Yes," she said, looking first at me, then out through the dirty windshield. "I've got to find it pretty soon," she said. ". . . Goodbye."

Then she drove off inland in her very dirty, very brown Thunderbird, toward whatever she was looking for, leaving behind a cloud of smoke that hung like a ghost above the street for a while. When she got to the end of the block, she turned left and disappeared behind a tall and fluffy eugenia bush.

4

Two days later, when I was cleaning up the shop and taking care of any business that had to be taken care of before I left, lo and behold, the infamous Vince McKelvey came in with a young, blonde girl who looked like the original surfer chick. She looked as if she was about eighteen, maybe even sixteen. Her hair flowed down all the way to her nice little butt and her short, cutoff Levis. You can never tell who is going to show up in a flower shop and for what reason. Things happen to people, and the first thing a lot of people think about is flowers. "Weddings, Birthdays, Funerals, Flowers for All Occasions," Pop always said. So here he was: Vince, Cindy Paquette's husband, the Cindy of "my pants were on fire" fame. He was a fireman, an ex-socialite, and he had curly blond hair and a cute button nose.

He had his arm on the shoulder of the surfer chick as she smiled a white-toothed smile and fondled his fingers.

"I bet you don't remember me," he said, cocking his head.

"Well, I don't know," I said. "You look familiar."

"I knew he wouldn't remember," he said, looking over at the surfer chick. "I'm Vince McKelvey. Remember?"

"Oh, yeah, sure. Vince. How's it going?"

"This is my fiancée, Tamara," he said.

She nodded and smiled again.

"We want to order some flowers for our wedding," he said.

"Sure," I said. "When's the wedding?"

"In three months," he said.

"My parents aren't here today, but they'll take care of it." Maybe, I thought. "Let me get you some pictures to look at."

Since the wedding was three months off, I figured I would take the order. I'd probably be back by then, or my mother would be feeling better, or my father might even get his head screwed on by then and head home of his own volition. Besides, we could always cancel on them if no one was there to put the stuff together, give the order to one of our friend's shops down the street. I didn't tell them any of this, of course. I just opened the drawer below the counter and pulled out a portfolio of Polaroids and other pictures taken by my folks of wedding bouquets and arrangements. Jesus, I thought, why did they have to come into the shop when Weird Cindy was lurking in the vicinity? I put the pictures on the counter between us and opened the page to the brides' bouquets.

"Beautiful," she said. "Look at this one." She pointed at a photo of a bouquet made of small, pink roses. "That's really pretty, Vince."

"You want white. White's for being a pure virgin, like virgin olive oil," he said. "Are there any pictures of white rose bouquets?"

"Sure," I said, thumbing a few pages back. "Here you go."

"Not that one," he said. "Man, that's just like Cindy had."

"Cindy?" I said.

"Yeah, crazy Cindy," he said. "Cindy Paquette. You remember. She was homecoming queen. I was married to her for way too damn many years. Your parents made the flowers for that wedding, too."

"Oh, I didn't know," I said.

"You were out on ships or something for a long time, weren't you?" he said.

"Yeah, I was on tugs, but I had a little accident, so I retired," I said.

"Don't you kind of feel like a fag, or something, working in a flower shop?" he said.

"No, I don't think so," I said. "It's just a job."

"I'd feel like a fag," he said. "Weren't you a cop in Playa

Grande for a while, too?"

She said, "Is there a different one with white roses?"

"On the next page, I think," I said to her. Then to him, "Yeah, I was a cop until I gave it up. I didn't feel like a fag when I was a cop, either."

"Maybe so," he said. "Anyway, Cindy went nuts, so I divorced her."

"Oh," I said, picturing Cindy's pants going up in flames.

"They had her in the booby hatch in Costa Mesa," he said, "but then they let her out."

Tamara pulled a piece of Dentyne gum out of her purse and stuck it in her mouth. Her braces glistened in the flat, florescent light. "Are there any other bouquets in this book?" she asked.

"Toward the back of the book," I said.

She went back a few pages.

"Those are some bridesmaids' bouquets," I said pointing them out.

"Those are really pretty," she said.

"It's no fun being married to a paranoid schizophrenic," he said "Believe me."

"Yeah," I said, "but that's pretty sad about her, isn't it?"

"She came after me with a gun and started shooting at me," he said. "That's a lot more than sad. The cops took the gun, even, but they let her out on the street after being in there just a month."

"We're going to have a maid of honor and two bridesmaids," Tamara said.

"So you'll probably need bouquets for them and some boutonnieres for the men," I said, "and you always get corsages for the mothers."

"It's going to be a really big, cool wedding," she said.

"Yeah, that's great," I said. "Lucky for you."

5

I should've known that Pop would take off to Mexico, or somewhere, before I'd left for Cinco Casas six months before. Back then, I was organizing things, putting most of my stuff in the one-bedroom apartment near the beach I'd rented from a friend. I was going to keep the place while I was gone. I even gave Dale, my friend and landlord, a year's worth of signed checks that he could cash when the date came up. It was a place I could call home, I'd figured, just in case I decided to come back for some reason and I needed it. And it was a place to get my mail. I could afford to pay the rent, since Cinco Casas was only a hundred and fifty bucks a year, and it was good to feel like a migrating whale with two places that I could go.

I was going to leave town to go down to Cinco Casas in four days. Jean had kicked me out of the house two months before, when she couldn't stand my being around all the time, and when we were doing nothing but arguing about anything about which we spoke to each other, all the time. If I said the sky was blue, she would say that it wasn't blue. "It's lavender." It had all started when she had shot me in the foot. I hadn't liked that much, and I wondered if she'd dropped it on purpose, just to finally be rid of me. But she couldn't have made the gun go off unless she had remote control, I thought. So that week before I left for Cinco Casas, I went over to get some of my clothes and books at what had become solely Jean's house. I figured to hell with the house. She could have it and the hundred grand that was left to pay on the mortgage. Dale had given me a good deal on the rent for the apartment, since he knew me and knew I was going to go down to Cinco Casas for a while, so he basically had

27

the rent for a year ahead of time.

I was putting some clothes into my van when Jean came out on the front porch and said, "Your mother's on the phone."

"Okay," I said. "Tell her just a minute."

I put the stuff in the back of the van, then went inside to the phone.

"Hey, Mom, what's going on?" I said.

"Your father's in jail," she said. Her voice was cracked and gravelly.

"What happened?" I said.

"He called and said he was getting some paint at Imperial Hardware and the security guard stopped him outside for shoplifting a lock. Oh, I don't know. I don't know."

"Okay, Mom, take it easy. He stole a lock? Something's weird there."

"He had your grandfather's gun and five thousand dollars in his pocket, the police said."

"What the hell was he doing with a gun and all that money?"

"I don't know. Call somebody down there and see if you can get him out of jail. I don't know. He's so hyper lately, I just don't know."

"I'll get him out. Take it easy," I said. "What in the hell was he doing with a bunch of money and that gun in his pocket?"

"I don't know."

"Okay. Take it easy. I'll get him out," I said.

Then I called the police department, got the officer on duty at the booking desk, and told him my name. Luckily, it was a guy named Manny Miranda. I knew him from high school. I knew a lot of cops from having been a cop and almost as many from high school. They'd always been the ones who'd had the most fights and the fastest cars to race, the ones who'd ditched school the most.

"Manny, do you have my father down there, Sabas Catalpa

28

Senior?"

"Yeah, he's here," Manny said. "I thought that that was your old man. He doesn't belong here. Come on down here, and we'll get him out for you."

"How much is the bail?"

"No bail. For some reason they aren't asking for any," Manny said. "They seem to think he's honest and he won't leave town, I guess. What the hell was he doing with all of that money and a gun in his pocket?"

"I don't know," I said. "Maybe he doesn't like banks."

"Yeah, maybe so," he said and laughed. "Come on down and get him."

"How much money did he have on him?" I said.

"Five thousand, six hundred bucks," he said.

"Jesus," I said. "I'll be there in a few minutes."

I told Jean what had happened and she looked at me, then around the room. She had a broom in her hands, and she leaned on it.

"What's he doing with a gun and five thousand dollars in his pocket?" she said.

"He always carries a lot of money," I said. "Maybe he thought he needed a gun because of the money."

"He stole a lock?" she said. "He had five thousand dollars in his pocket. Why would he steal a lock?"

"Hell, I don't know."

"At least the cops didn't shoot him," she said.

"That's good anyway," I said.

"One of these days you need to get all of your stuff out of here," she said. "When you aren't getting your father out of jail or going to Baja to sit on the beach and go surfin'."

"I'll get it all when I come back from Baja," I said, "promise. But I have to go downtown now."

"There's always something that you have to do," she said.

At the police station, Manny Miranda sat behind the olive green counter wearing a dark blue uniform, his chest full of medals. He had a manila folder in his hands that he was thumbing through.

"Hey, Manny," I said. "How's it going?"

"Not bad," Manny said. "Kind of busy, with people stealing locks all over the place."

He pushed the papers over for me to sign.

"I'll call down and tell them to bring him up," he said.

After a few minutes, another cop escorted him out from the back. My father was smiling.

"Hey, Pop, how you doing?"

"Oh, I've been better," he said, still smiling.

"You have everything?" I said.

"I have my wallet and my money," he said. "They're keeping your grandfather's gun on ice for me." He smiled, showing his gold tooth.

"I figured they'd do that," I said. "So is that it? Are you sure there's no bail?" I asked Manny.

"Nothing," he said, "that's it. It's like I said on the phone . . . Take it easy, Mr. Catalpa," he said to my father.

"I'll take it any way I can get it," my father said.

In the car, driving inland toward the shop and the house, the palm trees along the road waving in the wind, I looked over at my father, his blue eyes taking in the sights like whirlpools.

"So what happened?" I said.

"I was just buying two gallons of paint," he said. "And I stopped and put this lock in my pocket, then looked around for some other stuff. There was a bunch of other people getting things. A big line. They have a sale going over there. Then I went and paid for the paint, and I went out the door, and this young security cop comes up to me and says, 'So did you forget something?' And I said, 'I don't think so.' And he says, 'Put that paint down. You've got something in your pocket that doesn't belong to you, don't you?' I put the paint down and I said, 'Look, don't take this wrong, but I have a gun in my pocket.' So boom, he whacks me right in the forehead and knocks me on my ass. Next thing I know, he's cuffing me, emptying my pockets and asking me why I have a gun and so much money in my pocket. I told him I was going to the bank."

"So you were really going to the bank," I said.

"Hell no," he said, "I just told him that."

"Why did you have five thousand, six hundred bucks in your pocket?"

"I thought I might want to buy something," he said.

"What did you want to buy?"

"Who knows?" he said. "There are a lot of things you run into."

"And why the gun?"

"Because I had five thousand, six hundred bucks in my pocket," he said. "Why else?"

"That's logical, I guess," I said.

There was an old bar called the V Room on the corner just ahead, the big "V Room" neon sign above it, so I said, "Would you like to have a beer?"

"Yeah," he said, "a beer sounds good."

Inside, three old guys sat at the bar, a bottle of beer in front of each of them. There were no windows, just dim, fluorescent lights above the bar and the light from the jukebox. I ordered two beers from the bartender, an old pro who wore a white shirt and a black vest. My father sat down in a booth, and I paid the guy and carried the two beers over to the back.

"So how's your mother?" he said.

"She's a little freaked out," I said.

"That's normal," he said. "She's always worrying about something."

"You don't blame her, do you?"

"It's no big deal. They'll just slap my hands." He took a sip of his beer, then looked around the place. He had that young-looking face, without a wrinkle, the way he always looked when he was up and flying.

"I haven't been in this bar in years," he said. "It's still a

31

dump."

"So you put the lock in your pocket, then forgot about it?" I said.

"I didn't forget about it," he said. "I just thought I'd steal it."

"What was it worth, five bucks?"

"No, three seventy-five," he said. "On sale."

"You couldn't afford it, I guess?"

"Who knows?" he said.

"They might give you big trouble about the gun. You aren't supposed to have a pistol in your pocket unless you have a license. Anyway, you've got a record, and you're a registered alien."

"Don't worry about it," he said. "You're acting just like your mother. If they give me too much shit, maybe I'll go down to Mexico and take over the old hacienda. Get a whole bunch of horses."

"That sounds familiar," I said.

"You could come down to the hacienda, if you want," he said. "You like horses."

I sipped my beer and said nothing to that one. I had been hearing about it for my whole life. His father had been from a rich family, down in Jalisco, and he had been killed by a few guerillas before my father was born. He'd been a paymaster for the Federales, and the Villistas had shot him and then kicked his teeth out to get his gold fillings. The family had a lot of farmland and a lot of horses, and they owned the pharmacy, the hardware store, a bar, and the pool hall, plus a few other things in the village. My father had gone down there to Jojutlan before I was born, to visit the old relatives, see where he'd been born, and see where his father had come from, since he'd never known him. He'd gone to the door of the hacienda, he told me, and knocked on the door, and when his uncle answered the door, the first thing he had said was, "Oh, Sabas. Your grandfather had something for you, but I don't know what it was."

He always talked about that when he'd had a beer or two.

32

"Let's go home," he said, finishing off his beer. "Take me to my Mustang, down on Fourth Street. I'll drive home from there."

"Sure," I said, knowing that I'd follow him home, just to make sure he got there. He was flying as high as any red-tailed hawk could fly, once again. I should have known big trouble was coming down the track.

6

My Sicilian grandfather had bought the short-barreled clerk's Colt .45, vintage 1875, in a pawn shop in Chicago. He had seen a Colt in a movie starring William S. Hart called "The Man from Nowhere." Besides that, there was another story, that one of the sisters had seen a tie pin with a black hand on it in the cigar box where he kept his cuff links and rings and old watches. And yet another story was that two guys in suits had come to the door one night and asked, with Italian accents, if he was home, many years after they had moved from Chicago to California. One of the sisters had said yes, and then Grandpa came out and talked to the two men for a few minutes. He went in and got dressed up in his suit and got the Colt and his overcoat and his gray fedora, and he left with the two men, telling my grandmother only that he had to go, that he'd back later. And two days later, he had come back, walked into the house and changed his clothes, and put the Colt away, and after that, he had said nothing to any of the kids or to my grandmother about where he had gone. So they said that he went somewhere with two guys who were "probably in the Mafia" and that he had done something terrible with them. No one knew what that something was, but it gave the gun provenance, I guess you could say. He had kept it in a drawer for years after that, never shooting it, just cleaning it once a year or so, oiling it and then wrapping it up in a green flannel cloth and putting it back in the drawer, like his overcoat that hung in the closet waiting for a snowy California winter that would never come. Then the Colt had come into my father's hands. It was after midnight at the house, and there was someone pounding on the front door. My father was just getting ready for bed, and he was in his bedroom when the pounding began. Our neighborhood wasn't the barrio or the ghetto, but it was on the fringe, and it was a holiday, Mother's Day, and there was a lot of money in the house. I'd gotten out of bed and gone halfway down the stairs so I saw my father walking out of his room with the bedroom with his Winchester .30-.30, lever action, and he went to the door and looked out through the glass window. Outside, he saw my Sicilian grandfather, Paolo Vulcano, standing there and pounding, so he opened the door, the rifle in his left hand.

"Hey, what the hell you got a big gun for?" my grandfather said.

"Jesus, Pop. Come on in," my father said. "I thought you were some kind of nut out here, trying to knock the door down."

"I'm no god damn nut," Grandpa said, and my father opened the screen door for Grandpa, and he came into the house. He had on his gray fedora and his overcoat and his black, leather gloves.

"What are you doing out so late?" my father said.

"I got to get out of the house," Grandpa said. "That god damn Ginny, she's driving me crazy."

Ginny was actually my step-grandmother, but we just called her "That-Old-Bag-that-Grandpa-Married." She'd married him for the money she'd thought he had, because "only old, rich guys travel back to Europe for vacations." Grandpa was a bit of a Casanova, and he was old, but he was not rich. He'd met Ginny, the Hungarian woman, at a dance for old people like him and her, and he'd told her about the trip he'd taken to Sicily for a few months. He'd had on his gray fedora, his black gloves, his camel overcoat, and his blue, tailored Italian suit, and she must have thought he probably owned Italy, so she came after him and put her teeth deep into him, like some kind of Hungarian vampire. Grandpa was lonely, since it had been five years since our real grandmother had died, so he had, stupidly, asked Ginny to marry him. And that had been eight months before he came to our house with the Colt .45. It was the store clerk's model with the short barrel, good to put in your pocket.

"Sit down, Pop," my father said. "What's going on?"

"I got to get out of the house before I kill her, that god damn Ginny. That stupid woman," he said. "She's a son of a bitch, that woman."

He reached into the right pocket of his overcoat and pulled out the Colt .45, then held it out for my father. "You gotta take this before I shoot the son of a bitch," he said.

"Sure, Pop, sure," my father said. "You can sleep here on the couch. We'll take you home in the morning . . . You walked all the way over here?"

"She makes me crazy," he said. "I got to get out of that god damn house."

"Okay, Pop, everything is okay. Just get some sleep," my father said, then got him a blanket out of the cupboard and gave it to him, and Grandpa took off his hat and lay down on the couch, so my father turned the light off and went back to bed himself, taking the Colt with him, that gun whose cousin with the long barrel had been held in many gunslingers' hands. As I said, that was the gun that supposedly "Tamed the Wild West."

I snuck up the stairs Apache style, back to my bed.

7

I stuck around for Pop's hearing that time. He still had a green card, since he was a registered alien because he'd never wanted to go through the process and the humiliation of being tested on something like, "Who was the thirteenth president of the United States?" He'd been only three months old when he came to the States, so he was as close to being a citizen as is possible. Since he'd had a few troubles with guns in the past, it was a bad idea for him to go around carrying a Colt .45 in his pocket, no matter what reason he gave. He'd been here since he was one, but who knew what the government might do? Maybe they could call him an undesirable and deport him to Mexico. I had a lawyer friend, Johnny Matthews, whom I'd done a favor for once. He'd needed to have someone translate what a Mexican witness he was interviewing was saying into English. When my father was scheduled to have the hearing, I asked Johnny to come and help him get out of the mess he was in with the paint and the lock, and, of course, the Colt .45.

The courtroom walls were all mahogany, with mahogany benches to match. If there had been an altar there, it could have been a church. The judge was an old guy with wire-framed glasses and short, gray hair. He looked like Spencer Tracy. He looked down from the bench at Pop and Johnny, standing there in front of him.

"How do you plead, Mr. Catalpa?" the judge asked.

"I plead guilty, Your Honor, but with extenuating circumstances."

"And what are those circumstances?" the judge said.

"Walking out with the lock was an accident, Your Honor. I

37

just picked the lock up and put it in my pocket, because I was carrying two gallons of paint, so I forgot about the lock when I went to pay for the two gallons of paint to the cashier, Your Honor."

"And how do you explain the pistol you were carrying in your pocket?"

"I had a lot of money, Your Honor, so I was going to go to the bank, and I thought that I needed a pistol, because I was carrying so much money, Your Honor."

Johnny said, "Your Honor, he knows that he wasn't supposed to carry the pistol, but the pistol was given as a family heirloom to Mr. Catalpa's wife by her father, his father in law, several years ago, and that is how it got to be in his possession in the first place."

"Mr. Catalpa isn't allowed to carry a concealed weapon, no matter how much money he is carrying, unless he has a permit to do so."

"Yes, Your Honor," Johnny said. "He understands that."

"I see in the file that you have a history of having troubles with firearms, Mr. Catalpa."

"That was a long time ago, Your Honor."

"His son would like to take the pistol home with him, since it is a family heirloom," Johnny said.

The judge thumbed through some more papers in front of him, then scratched his head and said, "Okay . . . I'll release the pistol to the family, so long as they register it with the police. But Mr. Catalpa, I hope you realize you have broken the law and if you want to carry a concealed weapon, you must apply for a permit."

"I'll make sure it's registered," Johnny said.

"Yes, I realize what I've done, Your Honor," Pop said. "I'll be good."

"Are you being sarcastic, Mr. Catalpa?" the judge said.

"No, excuse me, Your Honor. I'm being very serious, Your Honor."

"You are very lucky that the hardware store isn't pressing charges for shoplifting, Mr. Catalpa."

"Yes, Your Honor," my father said.

So that had ended the paint and the lock episode. Johnny got him off, without probation or anything. It was miraculous, I thought. I'd stuck around town for a month to make sure that Pop had calmed down, and then I'd packed up and headed south to my Airstream on the cliff above the point break at Cinco Casas.

8

After Art had left Cinco Casas, I'd packed up and headed north to Playa Grande the very next day. I didn't really know where to go to find my father, so I worked in the shop for a month and tried to figure out where he might be, so that I could go into Mexico and get him out of trouble, if he really was there, before he made irreparable damage and trouble for himself. One night, I was at my apartment having a beer, and I answered the phone, and it was Cindy Paquette once again.

"They're trying to take my kids," she said.

She sounded as if she was crying. How she got my number was a mystery, but she had it. This was two weeks after she'd parked in front of my house. I knew she'd been in the mental hospital for a while, like Vince McKelvey had said, and he'd divorced her. They'd gotten married right after high school, since he'd knocked her up, and she'd had a daughter six months later, and then a second daughter a couple of years after that.

"Where are your kids?" I asked.

"They were here, and now they're gone with Vince and that god damn little bitch babysitter."

"Did the judge give custody of your kids to Vince?"

"That fucker always has them, but I had them, and he took them away again, so I have to talk to Brian."

"What's he going to do?" I asked. Brian didn't want to hear from Cindy again, that's for sure, so he'd changed his phone number, I knew that much.

"He's my friend," she said. "He can help me, like he did in geometry."

"You're not in geometry now," I said.

"But Brian can help me," she said.

"I can't give you his number. Jesus, I've got no time for this. I've got to go down to Mexico to find my father. Forget about geometry."

"But you can help me before you go away," she said. "Where's your father?"

"He's way down in Baja, I think, or he was down there looking at some old cave paintings in the mountains," I said. "I've got to go and get him. I'm really busy right now. Understand? And besides that, I can't give you Brian's number."

"You just don't want to help me and my kids," she said. "You're probably on the fire department, too. But you'll be sorry, god damn you, you big dick head asshole."

Then she hung up.

9

Four days later, my son Pete and I were ready to go down into Baja after Pop. Pete wasn't in school, so I told him I needed his company, and he said that he'd actually like to go. But when I came home to my apartment that night, the back door had been pried open and clothes, and papers, books, shoes, and everything else, were scattered all through the house, as if a twister had come through the front door and gone out the back. There didn't seem to be anything missing at first. It looked as if somebody had just wanted to make a mess of things. The TV was still there, and the stereo, and I couldn't figure out why anyone had broken in just to make a mess. A half-eaten peanut butter sandwich was in the kitchen, which was odd. But then I went into the bedroom and reached in the back of the closet, behind the shoes, where I kept the old Colt .45, and there was just the green flannel cloth that my grandfather had first wrapped it in. Why would someone come in and just steal a pistol? But I didn't have time to ponder things, so I picked up the clothes and books and didn't even call the cops. For some reason, I thought of Cindy Paquette. She could have been the one to break in, I thought. Now she might have another gun to wave around. How much damage could she do with that?

But I didn't have the time to worry about it. It had been a week since McMullen had come in and said he'd seen the old man, so I just closed the shop for a while, since my mother was too sick and depressed to take care of it by herself, if at all, and no one else in the family could, make that would, watch it. I even called Vince McKelvey and his bride and told them that there'd been a death in the family, that we couldn't fill their order, and that I'd give it to a shop down the street, which I did. Then I packed up and got my son Pete, and we drove the van down through Tijuana and south into Baja. Pete's first name was also Sabas, but to avoid confusion, we called him by his middle name.

The postcards and letters gave me some of the places Pop had been to and the dates when he'd been there. Driving south, we stopped and asked around at a couple of cantinas and restaurants that I knew he liked. They hadn't seen him, they said. When we got to Colonet, we went toward the beach and Cinco Casas and stayed there in my trailer for the night. In the morning, we surfed for an hour to wake up, then showered and took the road south again.

We drove the three hundred miles of desert, past tall, weird cactuses, and six hours later, we were in San Ignacio. From the highway, there was a yellow motel, then a dozen or so white houses, and then a half-mile square stand of palm trees, and beyond them, the bell tower of the church beside the zocalo of town. It was late October and seventy-five degrees by the thermometer on the dashboard of the pickup. Pete and I had just come across the Desierto de Vizcaino of Baja Sur. The mountains of La Sierra de San Francisco lay to our north. I knew that those mountains were where he had gone to look at the pictographs. I looked at the postcard from San Ignacio that I'd read the night before. There was a picture of the stone church taken from the zocalo just in front of it. It read:

Dear familia,

I am studying the pictographs of our ancestors in the Sierra de San Francisco. They are beautiful paintings that I believe represent the constellations. The Pleiades and Ursa Major mark my way, as they did the forefathers long ago. I'm following them. I'm going where they guide me.

Amor, pesetas, y tiempo para gustarlo,

Sabas Joaquín Gauguin, your Pop

I turned into the parking lot of the motel. There was a balcony with some metal tables on it and what looked like a restaurant that also had a sign, Oficina, above the door. I parked, and Pete and I climbed out. An old man who wore a straw fedora sat at a table on the balcony. He had a cup of coffee in front of him, and he was reading a leather-bound book that looked like a Bible.

"Have you stayed here before?" Pete asked.

"No, but it looks all right. And there's a place to eat."

"You think Grandpa stopped here?'

"Maybe. We'll see." An old Airstream trailer just like mine sat in the parking lot. Its long afternoon shadow fell across the dirt parking lot and the white van.

The old man looked up from his Bible as Pete and I climbed the steps toward the restaurant and the glass-paned doors that led inside.

"Buenos tardes, señores," the old man said.

"Buenos tardes," I said.

Inside the cafe, the walls were covered with posters of the Baja 1,000 and pictures of off-road cars and motorcycles. A man of thirty-five or so came out from the back. He wore a red t-shirt with Baja 1,000 on the front. I could smell something good cooking somewhere.

"At your service, señores," he said. "I am Ramon, and my father here is also Ramon." He glanced at the old man.

"We need a room with two beds," I said.

"Certainly," the young man said. "Perhaps you are hungry? We still have very good goat stew on the stove."

"We'll come back later," I said.

After we had gone to our room and washed up, we came back to the restaurant and ordered the stew and cold beer, and the stew was hot and spicy, and it tasted good with a beer after the long drive. The old man came out on the balcony again and sat where he'd been sitting before, two tables down from us, his black Bible still lying there in front of him. He was limping, and I saw that his right foot was bare and was red and blue and swollen. The sky was just getting dark now, beyond the grove of palm trees. The old man opened his Bible and began to read again.

We finished dinner, and the young Ramon brought out some flan for us, on the house, and the old man said, "Ramon's wife makes flan that is excellent."

I dipped my spoon into it and tasted it, and it was delicious. Then I asked the old man his name.

"I am also called Ramon, like my son," he said.

I introduced Pete and myself, then said, "It looks like you've hurt your foot."

"Diabetes," he said. "The doctors want to take the foot off, but I want to keep it." He smiled. "It still works some of the time."

"I understand that," I said.

"Are you driving to Cabo San Lucas, to see the beautiful women in those tiny little bathing suits?" Don Ramon said.

"I wish," I said. "Not this trip. We're looking for my father. A man at home told me that he saw him down here a few weeks ago."

"There are many old men who come here," Don Ramon said.

"My father has blue eyes and sometimes he wears a black Stetson," I said. I showed him an old picture that I had of him.

"An old man that looked like that came here," he said. "Was this man driving a big Dodge?"

"Yes, he was," he said.

"That sounds like him. Did he tell you where he was going?"

"He said he was going to Jalisco to get what his grandfather left him. Land and horses, he said. We told him about the old paintings by the Indians in the canyons, and he said he wanted to see them for his research. So he wanted a guide, and I called my cousin Ezequiel, and he came and said that he would take him. My cousin knows where there are paintings that nobody

45

has seen, and he says that there is Indian gold up there. So they went into the mountains, but they didn't find any gold. Ezequiel told the old man to maybe to get a good metal detector next time." He sipped his coffee. "He was glad to see the paintings. He said that they were important to him."

"Why did he want to see the paintings?" I asked.

"Quien sabe los norteños locos?" Don Ramon said.

"I didn't talk to him later."

"Is your cousin here now?"

"No, he's in Santa Rosalia for a few days, I think."

"Are there other people who know where the paintings are up in the Sierra?" I said.

"Certainly," Don Ramon said. "A lot of my family, the Arcos, is up there. They know the mountains as well as eagles."

We gassed up the van the next morning and got some water purification tablets and some food, and we drove back to the northwest thirty miles on the highway, then turned onto a dirt road where there was a sign.

San Francisco de la Sierra
45 kilometros

The sign was full of bullet holes. It looked like it had been there a long time.

The mountain in front of us was called El Caracol, the snail, according to our map. It rose up ahead like its name implied, the smaller mountains encircling it. The dirt road was straight for five miles, with not many ruts, and then the road began to climb and wind around, through the wheel ruts and around the arroyos and hills, past sparse pines with blue-green needles, and brush, and cactus, and yuccas, and many plants I'd never seen before.

"Why are we going up here?" Pete asked. "He's gone, not in the mountains."

"To ask them what he said."

"The old man said he'd left. Why don't we just go south?"

46

"I want to know why he went up here. Maybe it's important. He's been gone for a few weeks, so who knows where he is now?"

"He's just getting further away every day," Pete said.

"Maybe we can find out where he went."

"What could he get out of some old cave paintings?"

"There's no telling. Let's go and see."

When we got closer to the top of the mountain, there was a plateau for a couple of miles, then a village. It had a small white church in its center and a one-room school beside that, and in the surrounding hills stood ten small, white houses made of stone and plaster, with roofs made of palm leaves. Don Ramon had told us that two families lived in this village, the Arcos and the Barrigans, and that if we asked anyone there, they could guide us into the canyon. If anyone had come there they would know, since there weren't many visitors.

We stopped and parked between the school and the church. A man who stood six feet two or so came out of one of the little houses. He wore a white, straw cowboy hat and a white shirt. He looked like a Spaniard, not a bit Indian, and he had a black mustache. He walked toward us as we got out of the van.

"Buenos tardes," he said.

"Buenos tardes," I said.

"Can I help you?" the tall man said.

"I'm looking for an old man that came up here, a few weeks ago," I said. I described my father to him and showed him his photograph.

"A man who looked like that went into the canyon with my cousin, Ezequiel, as a guide," he said. "That was maybe three weeks ago. He was a very funny old man." He laughed and took off his hat.

"Did someone else go with him?"

"Yes. My brother. The man wanted to see the paintings, he said, so Ezequiel and Carlos took him."

"How long were they out there?"

"Maybe five days."

47

"Is it possible to go where he went?" I asked.

"Seguro que si," the man said. "Carlos is in his house, and he and I will take you to the canyons. We'll go for one thousand pesos."

"That will be fine," I said. We had bought some food in San Ignacio, and we still had some that we had brought from home. He looked at it and said that it was almost enough, that they had more food to take, and that they would pack it all, along with our bags and other gear, on their burros in the morning.

He led us to a stone cabin with a thatched palm roof, where there were beds for us to sleep. Beside it was another cabin with a kitchen and table and chairs for ten or twelve people. Raul was the tall man's name, and his wife, Guadalupe, cooked us a dinner of spaghetti with tomato sauce and some handmade tortillas. She was a thin woman with auburn hair, and she had a smile that showed that she had a missing tooth in front. She looked Irish with her freckled skin and auburn hair.

The next morning, after they packed up the burros, we mounted the mules and headed out. The food we had brought with us and our sleeping bags and gear were all packed on the backs of four burros. We all headed across the plateau, toward where Raul and Carlos, his brother, said my father had camped with Ezequiel.

"He said that he wanted to see the paintings to see if some ideas he had about them were right," Carlos said, then took off his straw cowboy hat and wiped his brow with his shirtsleeve.

"What ideas?" I said.

"He needed to see them so he could know about the past," Carlos said. He and Raul led the way down the narrow trail into the canyon. The mules danced down the trail as if they knew it well. We passed cactuses with thorns as long as a man's finger, and when we got to where the trail descended into the canyon, I looked down and saw the green stripe of palms, cottonwood trees, and laurels, and the silver glimmer of the sun on the creek

48

that ran down through the canyon's floor. It looked like a long oasis far below, and we all leaned back in our saddles, the front of our thighs pushed against the leather-covered ears that came out from the saddle horn to stop riders from sliding forward as we went down the steep trail that wound down the cliff.

When we reached the floor of the canyon, we stopped to rest and drink water in the shade of a cottonwood, and Raul and Carlos checked the supplies on the burros. We all stood in the shade, and Raul opened one of the packs and took out some tortillas and queso del rancho, and we ate the cheese with the tortillas and drank water from our canteens.

Late that afternoon, we reached the place where Carlos said he had camped with my father. Just the eastern cliffs were in the sun, and the place in the canyon where we stood was shadowed by the cliff above us.

"The paintings are up there," Raul said and pointed up toward the cliff in the sunlight above. "And there are some a few kilometers down the canyon and some more five kilometers down the canyon." He took his hat off and wiped his brow with his shirtsleeve. "There are many here."

"Some say that treasure is up there, somewhere," Raul said. "Maybe so. You need to get a very good metal detector, I think."

A few hours later, we pitched our tents, and I strung a hammock between two palm trees near where there had been a fire before. Raul and Carlos unloaded the bags and food from the burros and took the saddles off the mules to hang them on the low bottom limbs of some trees near the creek. They took the animals up to the top of the cliff, where there was grass for them to eat.

That night, at about one o'clock, there was a loud roar, then a hiss, in the canyon, and I yelled out, "What the hell was that?"

"That's just a puma, roaring because he's lonely. He is like your father. Everyone is always looking for something, it seems."

The following day, when we stopped to check the mules and the burros in the canyon in the shade of some trees, Raul came over and asked to see Pete's bota bag, and Pete took its strap from his shoulder and handed it to him.

"We have these, only bigger," he said.

"Yeah, where do you get them?" Pete asked.

"We make them from the stomachs of goats," he said.

"Show us one when we get back," Pete said.

"Certainly. We've had them for as long as I can remember."

"Does everyone up here have these bags?" I said.

"Someone brought them over from Spain a long time ago, I think."

"How long ago was that?"

"Oh, back when the Arcos first came with the Dominican priests, I think," he said.

"Does someone up here make these shoes, too?" Pete said. He wore short, leather boots that had soles made of tire-tread.

"My cousin Francesco makes them," Raul said. "They're good for walking in the mountains."

"I'd like to have some of them," Pete said.

"Francesco is old, so he doesn't make many lately, but maybe you can buy them," Raul said.

"Your ancestors back then probably saw the Painters when they came?" Pete said.

"No, I don't think so," Raul said. "The Painters had gone a long time before the Arcos came. Just the paintings were here, and I think that they were old then."

"How long have the Arcos been in these mountains?"

"Oh, a long time. Three or four hundred years, I think. We are still vaqueros, like the old ones," he said and smiled. "We live here and we make our water bags and our shoes and our lariats and do everything else that our fathers taught us to do."

"It's like the past up here," I said.

"Yes, just the same," he said.

As we rode the mules through the canyon, I thought about working in the shop with my father and mother, learning things in the shop, just like Carlos and Raul had learned things from their parents. I had started when I was ten or eleven, old enough to wire and tape the flowers and wrap the Easter lilies or poinsettias by the dozens, then carry them from the backyard to the shop during the holidays, where they could be sold as gifts for Easter, Christmas, or any other holiday or occasion that came along. I had watered the plants with a hose and the yard-long nozzle, making sure not to break off the flowers or bruise the leaves.

At the time my father was drinking a lot of tequila, among other things, since the business wasn't going well, my mother said, and part of the reason it wasn't going well was his drinking, and another part was his running all over the place with his guns and rifles in the back of the panel truck. About then we went night fishing with my father's friend, Blacky, a guy with black curly hair who'd been in the Marines in Korea and had a steel plate in his head as a souvenir.

"The best thing to use for bait's white bread that you ball up," Blacky said, "and then put it on the hook. Then you get this lantern, see, and you light her up and hang it off of the pier from a rope, at night, just above the water, and you reel out your line with the bread ball down there right into that circle of light in the water. The fish see it and they think it's a sunny day, so they school up, and bam, they hit those bread balls. Then you just reel them on in, nice and easy."

My father and Blacky and Art and I had stood there on the pier in the fog until midnight, our lines hanging down in the circle of light, and, sure enough, the fish had come to the light. You could see them swimming around like gold fish in a bowl, but they didn't seem to care much for Blacky's bread balls.

"God damn fish," Blacky said as he reeled in his line. "Bite, you s. o. b."

"They're not hungry tonight, I guess," my father said. He scratched his head, then reeled his line in above the water, opened the drag on the reel, and let his line and bread ball drop with a splash into the lighted water below the pier.

Just after midnight, the tide carried in something that from the pier looked like a big, white jellyfish. It floated by, beyond the circle of light that the lamp made below, and I could see what looked like a woman in a white nightgown, her skin as white as the gown. The swells and the tide carried her toward the shore. Someone went and called the police, and when they came, their red lights blinked while they waited for the body to come into shore, and when she was in shallow water they waded in and got her, then carried her out and put her on a stretcher that lay on the sand. We all watched the men from the ambulance put her on a gurney, cover her up, and then roll her into the back of their ambulance.

"She probably fell off of her boat," Blacky said.

"No, it wasn't an accident," my father said. "She wouldn't be in her nightgown if it was an accident."

"Think she did herself in?" Blacky said.

My father just looked over at Blacky and nodded his head.

The white ambulance drove silently away from the pier and down the street. The two cops sat in their car writing something for a few minutes, and then they turned off their flashing lights and also drove off.

We continued fishing, the pool of light below us in the water, the fish circling there and not biting. The fog came in, and we stood there with our lines down in the pool of light until two in the morning. Blacky kept talking about the lady in the white lace nightgown and who could have killed her and why they did it.

"Maybe her husband killed her," he said. "Or maybe her boyfriend."

No one caught a thing that night. And the next day, there were a couple of lines in the newspaper about the woman in white being found and about them not being able to identify her.

"She's just a missing person, I guess," my father said. "Maybe she was depressed so she just killed herself. It can get bad some times. Sometimes you look straight down into the abyss like looking down into a well, and there's no bottom."

He knew about that abyss, since he'd visited it a few times, I think.

Now my father was a missing person, but at least he wasn't suicidal at the moment, as the woman in the white nightgown had probably been. That's what I hoped, anyway. I knew that he had his down time, when he couldn't even get off the couch all day long, and there was no telling when that might come again. Now he was charging around in his four-wheel drive Ram, looking for Joaquin Murrieta, or Gauguin, or some other revolutionary, somewhere in Mexico or the world.

We climbed on foot up the trail that led to the paintings in the recesses of the cliff, and when we got to the top, we looked at the paintings of deer with arrows sticking in them, of whales breaching, and of men with their arms held up, one side of them red and the other black, and of women that were painted with breasts coming out from under their arms. It looked like the women had been spread open and pinned on the wall, like frogs in a class. These all were painted high up on the cliff so that it wasn't clear how the Indians had painted them. They might have made ladders or scaffolds to stand on, but some of the places where there were paintings looked impossible to reach. About then, I was starting to get down. Probably the moon, I thought. It had started on that first day riding in, and it seemed to get worse the deeper we went into the canyons.

"Some people found long leg bones near these caves," Raul said. "They say they came from giants."

"They got up there somehow," I said. "But giants?"

"Your father said they were aliens from another planet," Raul said. "That is how they got so high without ladders. Besides that, they could fly."

"Maybe so," I said, knowing that sometimes my father had some very strange ideas about things.

The next day, there was a cave down the canyon that had more paintings of mountain goats and deer, and we looked at the paintings, ten and twelve feet high and higher, some men with square chests, one half red, the other black, their arms in the air as if they were being robbed. Females who had breasts that came out of their armpits. Other figures that were painted with the head and body red on the left side and black on the right side. And some of the figures were completely red. Others had what looked like feather headdresses. Some figures had arrows sticking out of them, and we thought that they could represent the enemies of the Painters. Or maybe they were paintings of a time when the Painters had been attacked by someone who had killed a lot of their people. Whatever had happened, the giant figures were still standing on the cliff sides, as if they were watching and considering us while we considered them.

"How are you doing?" Pete asked me.

"I've been better," I said. "The further we get back into these damn canyons, the shittier I feel. I don't feel like doing anything but crawling into a sleeping bag."

"Well, you look like shit, too," he said, "if that makes you feel any better about being here."

Sitting around the fire that night, I took out a bottle of tequila that I'd brought along. I figured a shot or two would make me feel better. Raul got the metal coffee cups, and we had a few drinks while Raul told us the story of their family. They had come with the Dominican priests who came to build their missions. Their ancestors had come to protect the priests and to help them to build the missions, and they had worked at the missions along the way through California, which they thought then was an island. The people who had settled in the mountains had brought their skills with them, and they made the saddles with the wide ears off of the horn, as well as the large bota bags and the leather lariats, and their own shoes and clothes, when

54

they had to. The Arco family and a few other families who lived in the mountains had settled in where they could run sheep and goats and cattle, as well as hunt the deer that roamed the mountains. They'd called themselves Californios, and some of their family had gone with the Dominicans all of the way up into what was now California and the States, but others had stayed and settled there in the mountains of Baja. So the Arcos had been there in the mountains for more than three hundred years, with their few cattle and goats and very little water for anything.

"They saw the paintings back then," Raul said. They had asked the Indians who were living here then who had painted the paintings, and they had said that they didn't know, that the people who painted them had been there and gone a long time before they came. The Indians had also called them the Painters in the first place. He told us once again that they had found large leg bones that had shown them that the Painters were giants and they could fly. "That is how they painted the paintings so high on the rocks in the caves," Raul said.

They were very old stories that their fathers had been told by their fathers, however the Painters had painted the pictures.

"We are all poor in these mountains," Raul said, "but we are free, and we are happy living the old way."

Many of their young people had gone down the mountains to the towns on the peninsula, like La Paz, or they had gone to the mainland and Mazatlan, Guadalajara, or Mexico City.

"Sometimes they come back," Raul said. "Most of us are happiest in the mountains with our ancestors, I think. Maybe your father is happiest here with his ancestors, too."

"Maybe so," I said.

Raul said that my father had also liked to hear their stories about the old days of the people in the mountains, and of the Californios who still lived there.

"I don't care about the past or the paintings," Carlos said. "I just care about three things--sex, mules, and goats. I would like to be with a woman tonight, but, as you see, we only have mules and donkeys." He laughed. "Tomorrow I'll show you something wonderful," he said. "I think these Painters were very sexy."

"Sexy?" I said.

"You will see," Carlos said. "Your father wanted to take it with him, but it was too big for the mules to carry. Anyway, the government people would be angry if he took it."

Just before we got to another cave the next day, Carlos told us to come and look at a rock that was there. We followed him up another path, and then he stopped and pointed at a rock, three feet high and three wide. On it were carved petroglyphs of a repeated image, an oval with a line down the middle of it. I didn't know what they had carved there for a minute, but then Carlos smiled and said, "Maybe you have sex in the dark, so you don't recognize these."

I looked at the rock and saw that it was covered with ovals with a line drawn down the middle of each. There were maybe fifty or sixty of those ovals.

"This rock is beautiful," Carlos said. "It is my favorite rock in the whole world," he said. "This, amigos, is a magnificent monument to the vulva. What is more important in the world than that?"

10

The fire lit all of our faces, and the palms and branches of the trees around us, and it made my face and chest warm, that night.

"How did he end up in the mental hospital, that time when he had the rifle?" Pete asked.

"That was back when I was six," I said. "He went to jail because of his guns. He always loved his guns."

All of us sat in the circle of light, like fish attracted to a lantern. Raul and Carlos could only understand a little English, so they talked to each other while Pete and I talked.

"Was that the first time you remember that he did something weird?" Pete said.

"I don't know if I remember a first time, but this was way back, when he used to hang out at the bar across the street with Blacky and his other buddies. You know, some people are called crazy while others are just eccentric, so if they don't hurt anyone, who's to say who's what?"

My mother had told me about one time when Pop was flying high and hanging around with Blacky, who was always a little strange himself. Pop and Blacky had loaded the back of the truck with their rifles and pistols and ammunition and driven out into the hills to shoot at cans, or rabbits, or coyotes, or anything else they felt like shooting, the signs along the side of the road included.

One morning he was in the house with my mother, she told me, and he had his Winchester .30-.30, lever action, with him. He was hungry, so he was going to go across the street to the cafe and eat. He picked up his Winchester and went down into the shop, out the front door, and across the street to the cafe and walked in, rifle in hand. Grace, the owner of the cafe, and her son, Phil, told my mother later that he had sat down at the counter, then put the rifle right on the counter in front of him, as if he was an old cowboy and carrying the rifle to breakfast was something everyone did, something normal. Grace was behind the counter. She knew my father and mother, and she was their friend. She looked at him and his rifle, and she was afraid, she told Mom, but she went up to him with her pad and pencil as if nothing was wrong. Everyone in the cafe was quiet as they watched to see how Grace would handle this.

"What's the rifle for, Sabas?" she asked.

"Oh, nothing," he said. "Give me ham and eggs, over easy, with sourdough toast, please, Grace. And a cup of coffee."

"Sure thing," she said, then she went to the back and got on the phone and called the police. Grace brought him his coffee and eggs, and just then the cops showed up. My father took a sip of his coffee and looked over at the cops. One cop was a Mexican guy named Frank, and the other a black guy named Duke. Many years later, Frank and Duke would come back to the shop as customers.

"Good morning, sir. Please stand up and away from your rifle," Duke said.

Pop stood up.

Duke reached over and picked up the Winchester and cocked it and checked the breech, to see if it was loaded.

"Why do you have a loaded Winchester with you this morning?" Duke said as he handed the rifle to Frank, who stood behind him.

"I'm going to go up into the hills today to shoot at some cans," Pop said.

"Certainly you are," Duke said. "Put your hands on your head."

Pop did so and Duke pulled Pop's hands down and put some cuffs on him behind Pop's back.

"You aren't supposed to walk into a cafe with a loaded rifle of any kind," Duke said. "It's illegal and you make people nervous."

"It's just my Winchester," my father said, "and I'm not concealing it."

Frank checked the breech a second time and nodded his approval to Duke. Yes, it was positively loaded.

"I thought that it was legal to carry the rifle if it wasn't concealed," Pop said. "Hell, John Wayne does it all the time. "

"That's right. It's not a concealed weapon," Duke said, "but it's not okay if it's loaded. And besides that, you aren't John Wayne . . . Do you have any more guns or rifles around, Mr. Catalpa?"

"Not with me," my father said, "but I have some in my truck."

"Why are they in your truck?" Duke said.

"So that I can have them when I want them," my father said, "when I want to go hunting, or when I want to go and shoot at some cans."

"Where are you going to go target practice around here?" Frank said.

"I might go to the hills in Orange County," my father said. "You never can tell."

"Let's take a look in the truck," Duke said.

Duke and Frank stood there watching him eat, and my father said, "Mind if I finish my eggs?"

"Hurry up, we want to see what's in your truck?" Duke said.

Pop stood up, his eggs and toast half-eaten, and they went out and walked across the street, and my father went to where the old panel truck was parked. He unlocked the back doors and opened them.

There on the panel truck's wooden bed lay a couple of dozen other kinds of rifles and pistols my father had collected

59

over the years.

"Why do you need all of these guns and rifles?" Duke said.

"I'm going to start a gun shop," my father said.

"Sure you are," Duke said. "It sure looks like you have a good start on it."

So they took him to jail. He hadn't harmed anyone, but he'd scared a lot of people in the I. I'm not sure what the charge was, but it was probably something like possession of a firearm in public without a permit. Since he was a registered alien with a green card, it wasn't a good idea for him to carry guns around in his truck, or take them into any cafes along the way. It was obvious to everyone but him that he was acting crazy.

My mother got him a lawyer, and the lawyer had a psychiatrist examine him and diagnose him as manic depressive. From jail they sent him to the mental hospital in Camarillo, where they told my mother they were going to treat his illness. After many sessions of shock therapy, they made him a trustee, so he helped them bring others to shock therapy and, he told me later, he saw the people jerking from the electric shock as they lay on the gurney and realized what they had been doing to him for a few months. He either had to be there or in jail, and my mother thought the hospital was the better of the two.

From the base of the canyon, all of us had to climb up the hill and along a steep grade to get to some paintings that Raul was taking us to. At one part of the trail, there was a place where we had to step over a slide, where there were only scree and sand for fifteen feet. It was tricky to pass over it, because if you touched the loose rocks and scree, you'd slide down a hundred feet or so on a steep slope and either get scraped up or break something, or both. When we got to that cave, there were paintings of many animals and a few men on the ceiling of the cave high above us. One large painting was of a whale that was twenty-five feet long, from its tail to its head, painted as if it were breeching.

60

After we had looked at the paintings, we sat down on some boulders and ate some cheese tacos we had made earlier.

"Your father said he understood the stories that the paintings told," Raul said. "He said they made him feel good and he understood them."

"What did he say they were about?" I asked.

Raul took a drink of water from his canteen. "The stars, he said. And he said they are about hunting and the battles with their enemies."

"That makes some sense," I said.

"He said they were related to him and to all Indians and mestizos."

"That's probably true, too," I said. "How old are the paintings, do you think?"

"An old man found some burnt wood in a cave, and he said he had it tested, and it was from a fire that was built there three thousand years ago. He said there was a picture of a star that was exploding, too, and that had happened a thousand years ago. Your father said that he was probably right. They're very old, from way before Jesus."

"That's old all right," I said.

I thought about a day when I was maybe five years old. It seemed to have been a day that was very, very far in the past. My father had been drinking tequila all day long and probably all night the night before. But his eyes were clear and blue, and his face looked smooth, like he was twenty again, even though he was thirty-two. That's how he looked when he was high. Besides that, you could feel a vibration coming off of him as if he glowed. He seemed to vibrate with electricity when he was like that.

He and my mother were arguing about something, I remember, and he was yelling and swearing at her, his face red. I stood in front of my mother, probably trying to protect her from him, even though I was only six years old and three feet tall. A sword that he had bought somewhere in his travels hung on the wall above the fireplace, and he grabbed the sword, still in its scabbard, and, with eyes full of tears, he swung it high through the air above my mother's head, as if he was swatting a fly ball. The sword made a swooshing sound as it cut through the air. Then, apparently finished with his anger, he hung the sword back on the wall and went downstairs to the shop.

He was another man when he was flying high, and all of those things were in the past and indecipherable, like the paintings on the cliffs that no one would ever understand. No one knew or saw the people who had made them, and no one knew how long ago they had done the paintings there, or why they had put them there, nor how they had done gotten so high on the cave walls. There were no tall trees that they could have used to make scaffolding. There was nothing to make ropes with so that they could hang from the top of the canyon.

When we finished eating our cold lunch and we felt rested, we headed back down the trail of the canyon to our camp. We had set up our two tents, ours and Raul and Carlos'. My hammock was strung between two palm trees near the fire, and I sat down in the hammock and swung there for a while. Then I noticed the long-legged spiders. They were climbing all over the palm trees and trying to do a balancing act on the strings of the hammock. I whisked them off and lay back in the hammock to take a nap, but they continued to crawl off of the trees and onto the hammock then onto me. So I got up and went to the tent to lie down there for a while. But there, inside, the spiders had come in through the open door and were climbing all over our sleeping bags, like creatures in a nightmare.

"Let's get these god damn things out of here," I said. "They're all over the damn place. They'd eat us for dinner if we let them."

We took out the sleeping bags and shook and brushed the spiders from them. Then we went inside and with a couple of sticks started killing them. But when we'd killed what we thought was the last one, we'd see another spider, then another. They kept coming, as if they were very hungry and we were their dinner. They were like memories stepping out of the past. They crawled into the bags and up the sides of the tent, and they wouldn't go away.

Later that night, as on the night before, there was another loud roar and hiss that echoed down the canyon like a monster out in the dark. I figured that it was a mountain lion, as Raul had said of the roar the night before, but I thought of my father being out there and being in a kind of wilderness himself, just like the mountain lion, a place where he was a wild man on the prowl.

In the morning, I asked Raul, "Did you hear the weird hissing roar last night?"

"Yes, I heard it," he said. "It was a puma. Or I hope that it was a puma."

"Is there anything else that roars like that?"

"Maybe some kind of monster, but I hope not," he said. "The pumas smell the mules and the burros, and they're hungry. They probably think that we would be good to eat, too."

In another cave, there were more paintings of men and women with their arms raised and arrows sticking into their figures, as if they were the enemies of the Painters and these were painted to make magic and defeat them before a battle. There were also paintings of deer and mountain goats that had arrows sticking in them, probably memories of a hunt or wishes about a future hunt. Pete took a drink from the bota bag he was using as a canteen. It fit well on his side and didn't chafe or rub against him when he rode the mules or hiked up the canyon walls, and it was light, because it didn't carry that much water, which was both good and bad. There Raul looked at the bag and opened the stopper and squirted himself a drink of water.

We rode back through the canyon toward the trail that led up to the village of San Francisco de La Sierra the next morning, our last day there. We had to lean forward in the saddles going up the steep canyon wall so that we wouldn't slip off, and it was hard for the mules, since there were places where the trail was almost straight up and down. But we made it to the village in the early afternoon and, after they unloaded the mules, we got our bags and our gear and put it in our van. There was some beer in the cooler, and we got it out, and it was still cold. I gave Raul and Carlos each a beer, and we each had one. Raul went into his house, and when he came out, he had one of the large bota bags that he had talked about. It was black and shiny from use, and it had a square, wooden stopper. It looked as if it had been handled for a couple of hundred years or so. The design looked very old, as if the bag had come over with Cortez, but Raul said that it was only fifty or so years old and that it had just been made in the old style.

"My family has had these for a long time, from the old days," he said. "All of the people here have them. Your father said he would like to have one to put water in, so we gave him one."

"Did he say where he was going from here?" I asked.

"South, he said, to see family and more ancestors, and to get some horses. And to look for some more vaqueros," Raul said.

"Why more vaqueros?" I asked.

"I don't know. He likes vaqueros," Raul said. "I think that he wants to be a vaquero someday."

ii

We drove down out of the mountains to the main road and then to San Ignacio before dark, and there we got a room at Arroz y Frijoles, where we could rest and clean up for the trip south.

After we had showered, we came out to get something to eat, and there sat Don Ramon, in the same chair at the same metal table as before, his Bible in front of him.

"Buenos tardes," he said. "Was your trip to the mountains a good one?"

"It was a little bit good," I said "We didn't find out much about why he went up there, but we found out what he was looking at."

"Maybe you'll find out more later," he said. "My cousin is back from Santa Rosalia, if you want to talk to him?"

"If we can," I said. "Maybe my father said something more to him."

"I'll call Ezequiel," he said, and he went inside through the beaded curtain with the picture of the Virgin of Guadalupe on it, and a few minutes later he came out again and sat down. We ordered our meal of fish tacos from a girl with long, black hair. She looked fifteen or so, and her eyes were clear and dark.

"He'll come here, soon," Don Ramon said. "He says that he'll tell you what he knows."

When we finished with our dinner, a skinny man with black, greasy hair and a white mustache came up the stairs. He wore a black hat with a tin longhorn steer on the front of the band that looked like a child's cowboy hat that he'd picked up somewhere.

"Ezequiel," Don Ramon said, "this is the son of the old man you took to the caves. His name is Sabas, like his father's."

"Buenos tardes," Ezequiel said, and we shook hands.

"Perhaps my father said where he was going?" I said.

"Certainly," he said. "Back to the family hacienda with all of the beautiful caballos."

"I don't think that there is a hacienda or horses for him, anymore," I said. "That was all gone a long time ago."

"No," he said, "he said that his grandfather had many fine horses for him."

"The horses are just a forgotten promise, I think."

My father's grandfather had owned a big hacienda and a lot of horses, Arabians and Andalusians, but that was back before the Mexican revolution.

"He said that he might go to the Fiesta de San Javier, because he wanted to see some Indians," Ezequiel said.

"What's that fiesta for?" I said.

"It's for the salvation of all Indians. San Javier is their patron saint," he said. "The fiesta goes all this week."

The young girl came out to the table again and asked what we wanted, and we ordered beer for Ezequiel and us and a coke for Don Ramon. The girl went back through the beaded curtain and into the kitchen.

"What happens at the fiesta?" I asked.

"They have music and dancing, and they have people who sell many things," Ezequiel said, "serapes and tools and radios, perhaps. And there are games to play and food and beer. They have been having that fiesta for probably three hundred years. San Javier is above Loreto, in the mountains. The Indians come on a pilgrimage every year at the beginning of December."

The girl came out with the bottles of beer, the coke, and the glasses and put them down on the table in front of each of us.

"Gracias," I said. The light from inside the restaurant made long shadows of the beer bottles and the glasses on the white metal table.

"The Indians come from all over," Ezequiel said. "Mexico, and Guatemala, and even South America. I told your father that he could talk to many Indians who are excellent vaqueros up there. Quien sabe? Maybe he went up there to talk to them."

"We'll go and see if he's there or if he's been there."

"I think that you will find him up there," Don Ramon said.

"Did you go into the canyons to see the paintings?" Ezequiel asked.

"Yes, and we talked to Carlos. He told the same thing that you told me. He said that he knew what the paintings were about. It's a little crazy, him going up there."

"He's a little bit crazy, but he is a very amable crazy," Ezequiel said. "He is not a cheap pocho, I'm glad to say."

"No, he's the opposite of cheap."

"Exactamente," Ezequiel said. "Maybe you want to see some paintings that few have seen. I know of many good ones. We can to go into the mountains tomorrow. I have my mules and burros."

"Not now," I said. "Maybe another time."

"They say that there is Indian gold up there," Ezequiel said. "I told your father to come back with a very good metal detector and he could find it. No problem."

"These old guys really believe that there's buried treasure up there," I said in English to Pete.

"Do you think they're right?" Pete said.

"No, I think they're just about as crazy as your grandfather, but they seem harmless," I said.

"I have two thousand silver pesos, just like this one," Don Ramon said and pulled a silver peso out of his jacket pocket and held it up for me to see. "These are the old, good ones. Maybe you want to buy some?" He handed the coin to me.

"It's very nice, but no, thank you, Don Ramon," I said, looking at the coin. "I don't need any silver pesos right now. I just want to find my father and take him home." I handed the coin back to him.

"You will probably find him in San Javier," Don Ramon said as he looked at his silver peso. "Then you can come back and go into the mountains for Indian gold with him, perhaps. Maybe you will buy some of my silver pesos then."

"Maybe so," I said. "After we find my father, we can go and get the gold and silver."

"Will you come back this way?" Don Ramon said.

"Probably so, " I said.

"I'll bring some of my silver pesos here for you to see when you return," he said. "I know that you secretly really want some."

"I think that you should go into the mountains with me and look for Indian gold," Ezequiel said. "Don't worry about your father. He is fine and he will go home when he wants to."

"We'll go some other time," I said. "The treasure has been waiting for a long time to be found, and it can probably wait a little longer."

"Maybe so," Ezequiel said. "Who can tell?"

12

From Santa Rosalia, on the Sea of Cortez, we went south through Mulege and further south to Loreto. All along that two-lane road, we watched for the Dodge Ram that my father drove, and we there were trucks and Winnebagos and a few other RVs. The sea was blue and the sky was so clear that we thought we saw the mainland on the other side of the sea, but then we realized that it was an island ten or fifteen miles offshore. There were a few surfers with their boards on their racks. They were heading north, back to the Pacific side, where there were waves. It was a good time to travel, during the cool months of winter. We spent the night in Loreto and in the morning headed up to San Javier and the Fiesta de Los Indios.

All along the dirt road up the mountain, we passed peoplé walking, and we figured that they were doing penance or were on a pilgrimage. All of the people walking were dark skinned and looked as if they were Indians, or mostly Indian. Don Ramon had said people had been walking up that mountain path, doing their penance, for three or four hundred years.

An hour up the dirt road, we came to an arroyo where more Federales were parked, and one Federale in a uniform raised his hand for us to stop. I put on the brakes, and he walked up to my window. Behind him, a man wearing a blue guyabara shirt leaned on the hood of a black, four-door Chevy and aimed an M16 rifle at some ocotillo on the hill, while two other men wearing uniforms watched him. There was a half-empty bottle of tequila sitting on the hood beside him. He had a thick, black mustache and gray hair, and he looked to be the boss of the group. He pulled the trigger and pulverized the ocotillo up the road ahead of us. The man who had stopped us had an identical mustache. He leaned over toward the window, and I could smell the tequila and onions on his breath.

"Where are you going?" he asked.

"To San Javier," I said.

"What do you want in San Javier? Are you Indian?"

"No, I'm not. We're going to meet my father up there," I said.

"Why is he there?" he said. "He is not Indian, is he?"

"He's there for the festival," I said. "He's just a little bit Indian. We're supposed to meet him there today."

"Does he have arms to sell?" he said.

"No, he doesn't have anything to sell," I said. Who can tell? I thought.

"Do you have any arms . . . or drugs?" he said.

"No," I said. "We just have a little beer, and some water, and some food. Nothing more." I pointed at the cooler in the back. We had bought some more food and drinks in Loreto that morning.

The man shooting the rifle looked as if he was fifty or so. He stood up straight and looked at us, hiked up his pants, then stepped back and lost his balance before stepping forward and putting his hand on the fender of the car again. His face was red and he, too, was drunk. He lifted the rifle and leaned on the hood of the car again, then started shooting at a cactus that was full of holes, putting even more holes in its ears and knocking some of the ears off, one after another.

"Why is your father there?" the uniformed man said. "Are you sure that he has no drugs or arms?"

The man with the rifle shot at the cactus.

"Positive," I said. "He's been in Mexico for a while, and we're just arriving. Our family is from Jalisco and he wants to buy some land down there, he says. A lot of people in our family are still here in Mexico."

"Let me have your passports," he said.

70

"We don't have passports, just driver's licenses."

"Then give me those," he said.

I gave him our driver's licenses, and he stood looking at them with his red eyes. He nodded, then turned and walked to the back of the van, where he opened the back door, then opened our cooler that held our beer and water and fruit. I heard him moving things around in the cooler and saw him in my rear view mirror, holding things up and looking at them, bottles of beer, oranges, bottles of water. He came back to my window. "You were going very fast," he said. "Our radar said that you were going one hundred and twenty kilometers per hour."

"Radar?" I said. "What? You have radar?"

I heard the rifle's report again--pop, pop, pop . . .

"Of course," he said. He wiped his nose with his sleeve. "I should give you a ticket. But my jefe and my friends are thirsty, so why don't you just give us some cerveza?"

"Take a few cervezas, but leave two for us," I said. "We're thirsty, too."

He stared at me with his bloodshot eyes for a moment, then looked over at the man in the yellow shirt, who had the rifle, and the two other Federales in uniforms, who stood leaning on the other black car that was parked there. Then he went back and opened the rear doors and opened the cooler and fumbled around in it. The man with the rifle shot at more and more cactuses, and they exploded when he hit them. When the man in the uniform came back to my window, he was holding four beers.

"My jefe and my friends will be happy now," he said and smiled. "Maybe I will not give you a ticket this time. Go to the festival and when you pray, thank the saints for helping you." He stared at me as if he was waiting for me to argue with him as he handed me our driver's licenses.

Then the man in the blue shirt yelled, "Viaje!" and waved us on.

I started the van and headed up and around the bend as fast as I could without having them chase me.

"What was that all about?" Pete said.

"They were drunk on tequila, and they were thirsty, so they wanted some cold beer," I said. "It's called having the power."

"That's a shitty way to get a beer," Pete said.

"They'd just as well have shot us to get it," I said.

"Who do you think that guy with the rifle was?" Pete said.

"The Federale called him jefe, so I guess that he was a Federale, too, probably a honcho of some kind."

"I'm sure glad that they're all down here to protect us," Pete said.

"It's the past, down here in the frontera," I said.

"That's for sure," he said. "It's just like the Old West down here."

"I think that maybe it is the Old West."

Coming into the valley of San Javier, we could see the church its steeple at the end of the cobblestoned street of the town. There were makeshift booths all along both sides of the main street, the only street of the town, where vendors had blankets, serapes, films, music, shovels, tools, knives, clothes and toys. And there were other booths that sold tacos and pozole and tamales, ears of corn, and beer. The main street was about as long as a football field, and the church at the end of the street was made of black volcanic rock. People crowded the street while looking at the things in the booths and eating what they'd bought there. Near the church, there was a group of mariachis playing a corrido called Cancion Mixteca, and then they stopped and began to play the song that was about Joaquin Murrieta and his exploits, the bandit that my father always talked about. It was a strange coincidence. They were both songs that my father always asked mariachis to play, so I knew them. There was the Murrieta story where they had caught him and cut off his head, and then there was a story that he never really existed at all, that

72

the Mexicans had made him and his gang up so that they had a hero. And finally there was the story that he had escaped the rangers and lived a long life in Mexico.

We bought a couple of cans of beer from a stand, and we drank them as we walked along, looking at the stuff in the booths. People in the booths sold serapes and knives and candles and statues of the Virgin Mary of Guadalupe and Saint Christopher, along with statues of many other saints that I didn't recognize. We finally got to a church at the end of the road that was made of blocks of volcanic rock, and inside, there was a line of thirty or so men and women walking on their knees to the altar, toward the statue of a priest who was dressed in a brown robe. He was no doubt San Javier, the patron saint of the Indians. When they got to the statue, they kissed his feet and then walked to the pews and kneeled down to pray again. They all looked as if they were Indian--brown skin, black hair, dark eyes. I went over to where there were some votive candles and put a five-dollar bill in and lit three candles. I genuflected, then went to the back of the church to sit down in the back row for a few minutes. Old habits are hard to break, I thought. The only time that I had been to church in thirty years was to go to a funeral or to deliver flowers from the shop. But it was nice and quiet and very cool there in the church, and we sat there for a few minutes, watching the Indians as they walked on their knees, and we looked at the Stations of the Cross that had Jesus as a dark-skinned man, like an Indian, instead of a white man. Then I saw that behind the statue, there was a glass sarcophagus with an Indian Jesus in it. He wore a crown of thorns and a loin cloth, and his skin was dark brown.

"Who's in that glass box?" Pete said.

"I think it's Jesus."

"It's a little creepy. Wasn't Jesus a white guy?"

"Yes, I think he was. But they don't think so."

"Why are they all walking on their knees?"

"Penance," I said, "for being sinners. And they're probably

praying for divine intervention for someone, or for themselves."

"Do they think that kissing that statue's feet is going to help them?"

"Sure they do," I said. "That's why they go to all of the trouble of walking up the mountain and then come into the church on their knees."

"Maybe we need a little of that divine intervention?" Pete said.

"Maybe so. You can do some praying, if you want. I'm finished for today."

"Why'd you light those candles?"

"Just an old tradition that I continue," I said. "Your grandfather used to light candles for the dead and for good luck, I guess. You stick a couple of bucks in and hope for the best. You can think about that candle burning for a while. That's as much praying as I have in me."

"You did all of that Catholic stuff growing up, didn't you?" Pete said.

"Yeah," I said. "I was even an altar boy for a couple of months, but I wasn't much good at it."

"Why didn't you send me to church?" he asked.

"I retired, like someone said, so I didn't feel like sending you to those nuns and priests."

"So, am I just a pagan or something?" Pete said.

"Maybe you're a pagan. It's up to you. We thought we'd let you choose to be what you want," I said. "But maybe it was just a mistake. We probably should've sent you to those nuns, so that you had something that you could quit when you got older."

The line of Indians on their knees went out the door and into the street, and it kept getting longer. I figured that most of the Indians who were on their knees had walked all of the way on foot up the mountain on the road. Now they were walking on their knees, then kneeling in front of Saint Javier, who was the only one in the church who looked like a Spaniard, and kissing his feet, because they probably believed that he could help them get a chicken to eat once in a while, instead of beans and tortillas. I didn't get on my knees, nor would I.

A priest in a brown cassock came from out of the sacristy and passed the altar, where he genuflected and then walked past us to the front of the church, where the Indians were all in line on their knees, going up the steps and into the church. We got up and out of the pew and headed out through the doors, where the priest stood greeting people as they came in and went out.

"Good afternoon," the priest said to us in English, as he made the sign of the cross. Somehow he knew that we were Americans, or at least foreigners.

"Good afternoon to you, padre," I said.

"Are you enjoying the fiesta?" he said.

"We just got here," I said, "but yes, we are. We're looking for my father, but it looks like we're visiting Saint Javier and the church, too."

"Did he come here on a pilgrimage, to pray?"

"He doesn't pray too often, but maybe."

"Everyone is welcome here, no matter how long they've been away," he said. "I saw you light some candles."

"Yes, for good luck," I said.

"You should pray when you light the candles," he said.

"You're probably right."

"It's probably a sin to light the candles without praying, or it should be," he said and smiled.

"It probably is, like a lot of funny things are. I was just doing as my father always does," I said. "I haven't been in contact for a while . . . How many years has this fiesta been going on up here?"

"Oh, for more than three centuries," he said. "Many Indian people come here from all over to celebrate the Day of San Javier. They are all good Catholics, or so they say."

"Like I said, we're looking for my father. He wears a black Stetson with conchos on the band. And he has blue eyes and a limp. He'd be hard to miss around here."

"There was an old gringo here yesterday who had trouble with the Federales. He was a little bit drunk and he was singing along with the mariachis for a couple of hours. But he wouldn't stop singing, and he wouldn't let the mariachis stop singing. He wouldn't let them go, either. So the policia talked to him and then two Federales came and took him with them."

"Where did they take him?"

"To the jail in Loreto, I think. They have no office or jail up here."

"They took him because he was singing? Is that all he was doing?"

"He was giving a lot of money to the people that he met, a man told me. Maybe they thought that he was someone else, someone from the cartel, perhaps, because of all of that money."

"Was he wearing a black hat? Or any kind of hat?"

"I saw no hat. I just saw him singing and then the Federales talking to him and taking him away. But he was a gringo, I think. He had white skin, so he was no Indian."

"What about this man's car, a Dodge Ram. Did they take it?"

"I didn't see any car, but if he had one they probably took it down the mountain with them."

"That might have been my father. He's a very happy man, lately, and no doubt he's singing a lot. He's in a generous mood, besides."

"If you go down the mountain, you can check and see if it was your father. They will probably help you, if you treat them politely and give them a few dollars to help them remember."

"Thanks, it could have been him. We'll look around some more for a while, then go down and see if it's him they have in jail. Are you sure he wasn't wearing a hat?"

"No, I'm not. Is your father a little bit crazy, perhaps?"

"He wants to take California back for Mexico," I said.

"There are a lot of Mexicans who want that. They want to own Disneyland and Hollywood, I think."

"Walt Disney and John Wayne wouldn't like that."

"Perhaps not, " he said and laughed. "But they are dead, aren't they?"

"Yes, they are, but their children and their stockholders wouldn't like it, either."

"Probably not," he said and laughed again. "Good luck in finding him. I'll pray for you, since you haven't done so."

"That might help. Who can tell?"

"If you won't pray then I will pray for you," he said.

"Thanks for thinking of us," I said.

We went out and down the steps and left the priest and church behind us. That was enough church for one day, and that was about as close to praying as I wanted to get. So the Federales had taken a gringo to the hoosegow. I wasn't sure it was my father, but it sounded a little like him. We needed to ask around in San Javier some more. Anyway, if it was him, he wasn't going anywhere for a while.

Behind the church, there was a grove of olive trees, and among the trees, camps and tents and pickup trucks with campers. People were cooking over open fires in the shade of the olive trees. A big cloth banner was tied above a grandstand near the front of the church.

La Fiesta de San Javier de Francisco, est. 1679

There were only a couple of gringos or foreigners there in the street, and they stood out like lighthouses among the many dark-skinned Indians. We were hungry, and we had to eat before going down the mountain, so we started looking for a place to eat. Maybe someone else saw the man who got arrested up close, I thought.

We went down a narrow alley, behind the booths and the shops, and there was a restaurant with a dozen men sitting at the tables out front. They were all eating big bowls of pozole and drinking beer while they watched a soccer game on a small black-and-white TV. I was surprised they had anything on the

TV way up there in the mountains. There was no satellite dish that I could see, but there must have been one. Progress. We sat down at a long table where there were two other men sitting, and an old woman wearing a white apron came over to help us. I could smell the posolé, and it looked good, too, so we ordered two bowls and a couple of beers.

A young guy, wearing a frayed straw hat, sat at the table. He nodded, then said, "Buenos tardes."

"Buenos tardes," I said and then looked over at the soccer game on the TV. It looked as though they were both Mexican teams.

"Do you like the futbol soccer?" he said.

"I like it best when they make a few goals," I said.

"Futbol is very good game," he said. "It's the world's game. It's everywhere, like the Catholic Church." He smiled, then took a drink of his beer.

"Yes, I guess they have their presence in common," I said.

The waitress brought us the pozole and two Pacificos and put them down in front of us along with cilantro and raw cabbage and oregano and onions on the side to spice it up. We were hungry, and the steam rising from the pozole smelled wonderful.

The man in the straw hat finished his beer and so did his friend across from him. I caught the woman's eye and pointed at their empty beer bottles, then held up two fingers. When she brought the beers, they both raised their bottles to us, and we raised ours to them.

"To San Javier," the man in the straw hat said, "protector of Indians."

"To San Javier," we said, raising our bottles in salute, then taking a drink.

Just then, two more Federales in uniform drove by.

"More damn Federales," I said. "They're everywhere."

"You sound like you don't like them much," he said.

"No, not much. A Federale stopped us when we were

coming up the mountain, so that his boss could shoot up some cactus. The guy shooting the rifle looked like he was the jefe, anyway. Then the Federale helped himself to our beer."

"That was probably Peña and some of his men," he said. "He's the jefe of the Federales around here."

"Why's he shooting at cactus on the road to a religious festival?" I said. "They're drunk as hell."

"If it was Peña, he wants all of the Indios to know that he is the patron, even when they are praying at their fiesta."

"The Federale acted as if the beer was his to take."

"They have the guns, so it is theirs," he said.

"That's true," I said. "Did you see them arrest the man yesterday?"

"Sure. They arrested an old gringo," he said.

"We heard that. Did the man they arrested wear a black hat?"

I showed him the photo.

"He was way over there, so I didn't see him very well," he said. "But some people said that the Federales thought he was selling guns or carrying drugs, or trying to buy them. And they said that he was a gringo. But he didn't look like one."

"What does a gringo look like?" Pete said.

"They wear gringo clothes and shoes, and they have big cameras, and they're very rich."

"We're pretty much gringos ourselves," Pete said. "But we aren't rich."

"Yes, I know," he said, "but you're very amable gringos, I think."

I held up the picture in my left hand.

"This is my father. Sometimes he wears a black cowboy hat with silver conchos on the hat band. He might look a little bit like a gringo, but he's Mexican, from Jalisco."

"Maybe it was him. He was far away. But this old man was giving a lot of money to the mariachis and everybody else, so the Federales and the policia probably wanted to know why he was

79

being so crazy. So they talked to him and then took him away. He said that he was Joaquin Murrieta, but the Federales didn't think he was very funny. For them Murrieta is just another bandit."

"That's him," I said. "He has this idea that he's Murrieta."

The story was that they'd caught a man who they thought was Joaquin Murrieta near Fresno, in Central California. They'd chopped the man's head off and put it in a big glass jar full of whiskey. They'd also killed another man that they said was Three-Fingered Jack Garcia, a man with a finger missing on his right hand. They'd cut his hand off and put that in another jar full of whiskey. These prizes were the proof that they had finally caught and killed Joaquin and Three-Fingered Jack. But there were also stories after that, that the two men that they'd caught weren't Joaquin and Jack. So no one knew what had really happened.

"Why does your father say that he is Murrieta?" the man said. "Why doesn't he want to be Steve McQueen?"

"Steve McQueen?" I said.

"That way he could ride motorcycles," he said.

"That's true," I said. "But he's not big on motorcycles . . . We'd better go find him, whoever he thinks he is."

My father had read everything that he could find about Joaquin Murrieta over the years. When he watched "Zorro," or "The Cisco Kid," on TV, he told us, "Those stories are really about Murrieta. Every Mexican or foreigner has a little bit of Joaquin in them."

Joaquin Murrieta had been a topic of conversation in our family for as far back as I could remember. He and his friend, Three-Fingered Jack Garcia, were genuine bandits, not TV Mexicans who were almost bandits. They weren't good guys who helped everyone they ran into. Joaquin and Tres Dedos were supposed to have taken money and gold from gringos who were up in the hills trying to strike it rich during the Gold Rush any time they had the chance, and then they had supposedly given the money and gold to peons and Indians. Along the way, Joaquin and Jack had killed a lot of gringos, so the gringos did not like them much.

It was said that Joaquin Murrieta had come to San Francisco on a ship from Mexico during the Gold Rush with his wife, Carmelita, and his brother. They had gone into the hills to find a good claim, and they found a good spot where there was some gold along a river, and he and his brother had started to dig and pan for gold there, near Mokelumne, in the foothills of the Sierra Nevada. They found some gold at their claim and took it to town and had it weighed and assayed, and a few nights later some gringo miners had come and taken his wife and raped and killed her, and they had lynched his brother, so Murrieta had gone crazy for a while. Then he had become a bandit, raiding camps and villages and towns throughout California and taking his revenge out on any gringo that he ran into on the road.

Along with that, his friend, Three-Fingered Jack Garcia, or Tres Dedos as they called him, had the bad habit of killing Chinese men and collecting their braided queues to then dangle them from his saddle horn as prizes. I guess Murrieta and Garcia and his men wanted to take California back for the Mexicans, but it hadn't worked out well for them, since they were a group of only six or seven men, and the gringos kept coming and coming to look for gold in the hills. There were a dozen or more bandits who called themselves Joaquin at the time, so Murrieta was often blamed for raids that happened on the same day and at the same time, several hundred miles apart.

A former Texas Ranger, Captain Harry Love, and his men, all deputized as California Rangers by the governor, were sent out to capture or kill Joaquin, Jack Tres Dedos, and his band. After many months, they cornered and then killed a man that they thought was Joaquin near Fresno, along with Three-Fingered-Jack Garcia, and they took the jars back to San Francisco, where they could then collect the bounty of five thousand dollars. Yet even after Murrieta was pronounced dead, there were still reports of some who called themselves Joaquin Murrieta and Jack Garcia robbing and killing gringos and Chinamen, and anyone else in California who got in their way. Lucky for us, even though my father had it in his head that Joaquin was our relative, he at least hadn't followed in Joaquin's footsteps. He wasn't killing or robbing anyone. He may have thought about it, when he was very wacko, but he was really nothing but a nice guy to everyone, gringo or otherwise, even though he was crazy. Instead of robbing everyone, he gave friends and clients that he liked tamales or plants at Christmas and Easter. Of course, there were people who said that Joaquin Murrieta never existed, that people had made him up and that he was only a combination of several Joaquins who were robbing people in California at the time. It could have been the gringos who made up the story, because they wanted to give all Mexicans and foreigners a bad name. Or it could have been the Mexicans, who wanted to have someone who was on their side, fighting for them.

We walked all around San Javier for an hour longer, looking for Pop's old Dodge Ram. There was only the main street with narrow alleys behind the buildings on each side, so we walked the whole village and looked at all there was easily. If it was Pop that the priest and the man in the cafe had seen get arrested, then either the Federales or someone else had taken his car, too. When we were done, we got in the van and bumped down the dirt road, through the wheel ruts, toward Loreto and the Federales' jail, to see whoever it was that they had in their cell.

The Federales' office and jail had two dead eucalyptus trees out front, their leaves as brown and weather-beaten as old rope. Inside, a Federale with a mustache like Generalisimo Franco stood behind a tall, black desk. He was smoking a cigar and writing something down in a black ledger.

"Pardon me, señor," I said, "do you have an old man

named Sabas Catalpa in your jail? We were told that he might have been brought here. They arrested a man who might him be him in San Javier."

"And your name is?" he said then took a drag on his cigarette.

"I'm Sabas Catalpa, too," I said. "And this is my son, another Sabas Catalpa."

"Why do you have Mexican names? You are gringos, no?" he said.

"We're Mexican gringos," I said.

He looked us over, then licked his finger and turned the pages of his ledger. I figured that few people, if any, had been arrested in San Javier or in Loreto during the past day, but he looked through his ledger as if they'd hauled in dozens.

"There was a man who at first called himself several names, who was questioned yesterday," he said. "He said that he had lost his identification, and he told us that his name was once Joaquin Murrieta. Then we found his papers in his car and saw that he was lying, that he was really Sabas Catalpa. I think he is a little bit loco. But we found no contrabando, so we let him go this morning. Do you know who Joaquin Murrieta is?"

"He was a bandit in California, a long time ago, during the Gold Rush. He's been dead a long time. What time did you let him out?"

He looked in his ledger again. "Ten this morning," he said.

"Do you know where he went?" I said.

"We are not a travel agency, señor," he said. "We had his car, and we gave it back to him, and then he drove away. That is all we know."

"Is there anything else you can tell us?" I said.

"No. That is it," he said.

"Too bad," I said. "We thought that we'd caught up to him."

We turned to leave.

"Just one minute," he said. "Do you two have any armas

or drogas?"

"No," I said, "we don't have anything like that."

"Maybe your father gave you his arms and drugs?" he said. "Maybe you are really this Joaquin Murrieta."

"No, not me. My father just says that sometimes. He likes Murrieta, so he likes to joke around about it. But he didn't give us anything, because we never even saw him."

"I will look in your car to see if you have any contrabando," he said.

Once again, I thought. "Please take a look."

"Perhaps I will find something? Perhaps you are both bandits."

"It's not us," I said. "Murrieta's been dead for a long time."

He went to the side door of the van and opened it, then opened the ice chest. He wouldn't find more than four or five beers there, since we had drunk a few and the Federale on the road had taken most of the rest. This cop reminded me of a few cops I'd known when I was in that club for that terrible year and a half. Some of them just loved putting people in jail. You weren't just a brother or a friend. You were a cop, with all the dressings, and even if you weren't a pendejo, everyone thought that you were.

Outside, the cop opened the back door of the van, lifted up the boards and looked under them, and then opened the cooler and looked inside it.

"Maybe you are carrying gringo beer?" he said. "Maybe Bud Lite?"

"No, we just have a few Mexican beers," I said. "Three Tecate and two Pacificos, as you can see."

"Maybe there is something besides beer in these bottles," he said, grabbing a bottle of Pacifico and pulling it out to look at it in the sun. "Maybe I have to send these bottles to be tested."

"Please," I said, "take all of the beers and have them tested." This guy probably has radar too, I thought.

84

"Do you have your papers?" he said. "Visas de turismo?"

"Only driver's licenses," I said.

"Let me see them, please," he said.

We gave him our licenses. He took them and took out a small spiral notebook from his back pocket, then wrote in it. "Where are you going from here?" he said.

"Down to La Paz," I said.

He looked at us, his eyes just slits, since the afternoon sun was behind us.

"You can go," he said, as he handed back our licenses. "These are very dangerous times in Mexico. Be very careful. The Federales and the policia and the army are watching everyone who is suspicious for contrabando."

"Yes, señor," I said, "thank you very much." I wondered if there were ever times that weren't dangerous in Mexico, since I'd never heard of any.

As we drove away, I looked in the mirror and saw him writing something else down in his notepad, probably our license number.

"That guy really wants to arrest somebody today," Pete said.

"Some cops will arrest anyone that they can get their hands on," I said. "I've known a few of those over the years."

"So where do you think Grandpa went?"

"South, I guess. Maybe we can catch up with him now. We were close."

"This stuff about vaqueros and Joaquin Murrieta sounds pretty damn crazy," Pete said. "I sure hope that I'm not going to go wacko when I'm older."

"Who knows?" I said. "Maybe it's fun to be wacko."

"I mean because of genetics," he said.

"I figure it's the same as being born with blue eyes. Only it makes you nuts. And you have blue eyes, don't you?"

î3

Driving south, I told Pete as much as I knew about the family in Jalisco and what had gone on about the time when my father was born. My father had told me what had happened to my grandfather during the revolution. My grandfather had been a Federale, a paymaster who carried money from place to place to pay the federal troops. One morning, he and two soldiers rode over a hill on their horses in Michoacan and ran right into a bunch of Villa's men. The Villistas killed my grandfather and the other men and then kicked their teeth out to collect the gold fillings. And, of course, they also took the soldiers' pay he was carrying. That was what they were after in the first place. This had been when my grandmother was still pregnant with my father, near the end of the revolution. When my father was born, my great-grandfather told my grandmother to come to Jojutlan and live with the Catalpa family. He and the other Catalpas would take care of her and his grandson, he said.

My grandmother decided my great-grandfather was going to take my father away from her, so she was afraid of him. My great-grandfather had a lot of land, a lot of horses, and a lot of money, so he was the number one patron around Jojutlan. She had nothing but a baby boy with a club foot, so she had taken the train north to Mexicali to get away from him and from the revolution and Mexico. All along the train tracks, the telegraph and telephone poles had men hanging from them, revolutionaries that the Federales had captured and killed. On every train station wall, there was a long line of bullet holes, chest-high. It was seventeen hundred miles of men hanging from the telegraph poles, with an occasional woman hanging there, too, along with thousands of bullet holes in the walls of one station after another and one telegraph pole after another. The dead hanging there must have looked like Spartacus and his army of slaves along the Appian Way, after they'd been caught and crucified.

She'd gone to California, to a little house with an outhouse behind it, the house where her sister lived, in the middle of the orange groves and strawberry fields. That was back when there were still orange groves and tomato fields everywhere. So my father had been brought up there, in what they called La Colonia.

Just before I was born, my father had gone back to Jalisco to see his family there, he told me. He knew very little about them, only that they had been rich and had lived in Jojutlan, on Lake Chapala, for three or four hundred years. When he got to Guadalajara, he got a place to stay and then put on his suit and drove the fifty or so miles to Jojutlan. There he went to the town's zocalo and was told that the Catalpa family had a house right there on the square. He went to the door of the house and knocked, and a man of sixty or so came to the door.

"Good day, señor. My name is Sabas Catalpa. I'm looking for someone from the Catalpa family."

"Oh, Sabas, it's good to finally see you. I am your uncle, Efrain," the man said. He was my grandfather's brother. Efrain hugged my father. Then, before he invited him in, he said, "You know, my father had something for you, but I don't know what it was."

Then I told Pete about one night when my father was acting loco. He and Blacky wanted to go out and shoot at something. I was eight years old then. At the time, a lot of the dairy farms and orchards and strawberry and tomato fields on rural land were being bought up by housing tract developers, so the barns and fields were abandoned and ready to be bulldozed to make room for the carpenters and the rows of identical tract houses. This was after the Second World War and the Korean

War, when all of the sailors and marines and army guys had passed through California on their way to both wars in the Pacific and decided they liked the place and the weather. Houses were being built in a lot of one-horse towns that had been mostly orange groves, tomato, strawberry, and bean fields, and dairies. That had happened to a little town called Artesia, ten or fifteen miles from the coast and Playa Grande. It was about half an hour's drive inland from our house and the shop. The old barns and the milking sheds held only mice, rats, crows, and big barn owls that fed on the mice and rats. Pop and Blacky got a couple of twenty-two hex barrel rifles, a few boxes of ammunition, and some flashlights, and they and my brother and I all headed out to one of the abandoned dairy farms. Pop and Blacky figured they could find some barn owls, or something else they could shoot at, out there. It didn't make much sense to shoot barn owls, since they weren't birds you could eat and they hurt no one and kept the rat and mice population down, but there was little else nearby to shoot within forty or fifty miles. My father and Blacky were drinking a lot of tequila and running wild, so when they had heard from my Uncle Harry that owls were out there in the abandoned dairy farms near Harry's house and his housing tract, they were ready to go hunting.

At sunset, they loaded up the truck with rifles, ammunition, beer, and burlap sacks to carry the owls in, if they shot any. They bought a couple of six packs of beer and a bottle of tequila and loaded that in there, too. A new housing tract was going to take the place of that abandoned dairy farm. I was eight years old, and my brother was five, but my father brought us along with him on his big hunt.

When we got there that night, Blacky and my father got the rifles and flashlights out of the back of the truck and we all climbed over a rusty old barbed wire fence that surrounded the old dairy. The weeds were knee-high, and there was a moon out, so as we walked along with our flashlights, we could see the dark shapes of the barns and other buildings in the moonlight. We walked through weeds that rustled and cracked beneath our feet as we went trudged through them. That sweet smell of cow manure was still there.

"They'll be up on those telephone poles, or in the barns," my father said as we walked along through the brush.

"You can walk right up to them," Blacky said. "They think that no one can see them, because of their camouflage."

"Why are you going to shoot owls?" I asked.

"We want to hunt something," my father said. "We need practice."

"Is it fair?" I said.

"Of course it's fair," he said. "We're hunters, so we hunt things."

His face looked young, like it always did when he was flying high, and you could feel his energy when you got close to him, as though he gave off electricity and sent out vibrations all around him, like a microwave oven.

We walked into the big, open door of a barn. When we got inside, my father shined the flashlight around in the rafters as he looked for any owl that might be there. High up in the rafters, there was a shape with orange eyes that shone when the light shone on them.

"There's one," my father said as he handed me the flashlight. "Hold the light on him," he said.

I took the flashlight and shined it on the owl perched up in the rafters, and my father raised the .22 rifle and aimed and shot. The owl fluttered for a moment, then fell to the ground with a thud, and a few feathers drifted down toward the ground like big snowflakes. Pop went over and picked the big bird up by a wing, then put it in a gunnysack.

Outside, he shined the flashlight up at the telephone poles as we waded through the weeds. Another owl's eyes shone up on a cross beam, and Blacky raised his rifle and shot, and that owl fluttered down to the ground, where it beat its wings on the dirt for a moment, then stopped. Blacky went over and picked up his owl and put it in another gunnysack. We kept walking and shining the lights up into the rafters of another barn, then another. But no other owls appeared in the flashlight's beam. "Our shots must have scared them off," Pop said.

"We'd better get the hell out of here," Blacky said. "Somebody might call the cops."

"No, they won't. They'll just think it's some cowboy movie on TV," my father said. "Anyway, screw the cops. What business is it of theirs? We're hunting. We're hunters."

"Yeah, I guess so," Blacky said.

My father and Blacky carried the gunnysacks with the birds in them back through the weeds to where the car was parked, and they put the sacks in the trunk along with the rifles.

On the way home, Blacky sat in the front, riding shotgun, and Art and I sat in the back. The radio was playing Mexican music with a lot of horns tooting and guitars strumming so that it was hard to hear what anyone was saying.

"Now what are we going to do with them?" Blacky said.

"Maybe we'll get them stuffed," my father said. "They'd look good sitting on a shelf on a fireplace."

"Nobody will stuff them. I think it's illegal to shoot them. They're some kind of special owl."

"Why didn't you say something?"

"I was more worried about the bad luck part," Blacky said.

"What bad luck part?"

"It's bad luck killing owls. That's what my Cherokee grandfather told me back in Oklahoma. They're some kind of messengers of bad news."

"Why in the hell didn't you say something?" my father said.

"I figured you knew, and I figured we wouldn't find any owls anyway."

"How would I know it's unlucky? I'm a Mexican, not a Cherokee. I wouldn't have shot the damn things if I'd known it was bad luck."

"Oh, it's probably nothing to worry about," Blacky said. "Just some old Cherokee story."

"It's bad luck, and you didn't say anything?"

"I figured that you didn't give a shit," Blacky said.

"I don't give a damn if it's legal or not. But being unlucky's something different."

The next morning, Pop got a shovel and dug a three-foot deep hole in the ground behind the house. He got two tall, galvanized cans that he put flowers in and buried the birds deep in the ground. He didn't want anyone else to see what they'd done, so he was burying the evidence. He packed the earth down on top of them. Then he made the sign of the cross and mumbled something in Spanish and made the sign of the cross again.

"Okay," he said, "now they're buried nice and religious, so they won't bring bad luck."

"Why do they bring back luck?" I said.

"I don't know," he said. "But Blacky says they do. You heard him. It might just be some old Cherokee wives' tale, but no sense inviting trouble."

Three weeks later, my mother went to the hospital for some mysterious reason, so my father took Art and me downtown to see "The Gun Fight at the O.K. Corral," where Wyatt Earp and his brothers shot it out with the Clantons, their guns and rifles smoking, while Art and I wondered where our mother was.

That night, on the way home in the station wagon, Pop said, "You were right about killing those owls that night. I shouldn't have done that. That was really stupid. I don't need bad luck."

Twenty years later, my mother told me that she'd had a miscarriage that night, and that it had been a girl, on that night we'd watched the Gun Fight at the O.K. Corral.

Two weeks after burying the owls, I heard the cash register ring while my father was in the house getting a cup of coffee. I peeked out through the screen door and saw a guy who looked like my father's half-brother with his hand in the cash register. Then he saw me, and he turned and ran out the door. I ran into the house and told my father what had happened, and my father ran out to the station wagon and went down the dark street after him, but whoever it was got away.

The next day, my father drove me downtown to the green building that was the police station to look at a lineup of guys the police had in jail. I stood there, twenty feet away from six dark-skinned men, a short guy, a tall guy, a skinny guy, a fat guy, a guy with curly hair, a guy with a flat top.

"Do you recognize anyone here?" a cop said.

"No, he's not here," I said.

I didn't tell them who he had looked like.

A month later, Pop got in an accident and totaled the Mercury with the twin pipes he loved to rumble as he took off down the street. Then business was bad for a month. No one came in and ordered a casket spray, a regular spray, or an arrangement for a funeral. No young bride came in with her mother or husband to order wedding flowers. No one ordered flowers for people who were in hospitals.

"Business stinks," my father said. "I bet that it's those damn owls and that hex Blacky was talking about. What in the hell was I thinking?"

During those years, Francesco, or Franky, my father's half-brother, was in a car club called the Persians in Wilmington, a town nearby that was full of Chicanos and Mexicans and Filipinos and Blacks and Japanese who worked on the docks or in the fish canneries. Franky drove a lowered black Mercury with black-and-white angora dice hanging from the rearview mirror. He came by one day to talk to my father about something, and I looked at him and still thought that he had been the robber. If not, it was someone who looked a lot like him.

The next Sunday morning, after all of those bad things had happened, my father went into the backyard and dug up the two owls in the galvanized cans, then took them and me and drove into the hills in Orange County, near a cemetery where many people in my father's family were buried. On the yellow hill behind the cemetery, he waded into the tall grass with the two cans, put them down, and dug a hole three feet deep, as he had done before, then sprinkled the owls with holy water he'd gotten from a church somewhere, lit a gray twig of sage on fire, and made the sign of the cross with the smoke. Then he buried them and put a small wooden cross up to mark their grave.

Everything seemed to go bad. My father was on a losing streak. He could just lie on the couch then, unable, it seemed, to stand and work or go shooting, or do anything, in a long stretch of depression that was like fishing for tuna in a dry desert. He had cussed the owls and kept going to church and lighting candles. He had blamed God and the devil. He had blamed everything but the chemicals that flowed through his synapses.

14

Pete drove south, through more Baja desert, past tall cactuses and other cactuses that looked like elephant legs, toward La Paz. Miles Davis was playing "Sketches of Spain." Pete didn't say anything for a couple of hours, and I slept on and off.

When I woke up, Pete said, "Was your father always nuts?"

"Not always. Once he was fine for fifteen years."

"Did he ever get mean?" Pete said.

"Sure," I said, "sometimes, but he was also funny sometimes, too, in a weird way."

On that night, the whole family had been at Jean's and my house--Mom and Pop, and Art and his wife and kids, and Jean and our kids. We were celebrating both my mother's and my father's birthdays. We always did it that way, since they were only two days apart. Pete had only been seven years old then, so he didn't remember much about it now. But Pop was really flying at the time. He'd been running like a cheetah for six months or so, and, as always, his face was different, all of the wrinkles disappearing so he looked twenty years younger than he really was. He paced back and forth from the kitchen to the living room and sipped his cup of coffee, then paced back and forth some more.

"I've got to go and get some gas," he said. "See you in a minute. They might close early on Sunday. You never can tell."

"We can get gas later," my mother said. "We're going to open the presents in a minute. Have some of this cake and ice cream."

"Later. I'll be right back," he said. "I have to make sure I get some. Don't worry about it."

"Okay, I won't worry," I said, "if you stick around?"

"It's getting late," he said. "I've got to go."

He went out the door, and we all looked at each other, all of us apparently aware that he was looking for trouble out there, even if it was his birthday.

During that time, we tried every reason that we could think of to make him go to a doctor, but he said, "I feel perfect. What the hell do I need a doctor for?" But my mother had gotten together with their family doctor, who had given her some lithium that she was supposed to put in his food to try and bring him down a notch or two. She'd sprinkle some of it in his vanilla ice cream, which she made sure he ate every night. But even though she had been salting his ice cream with lithium, he was still flying high with the hawks and running with the mountain lions.

Ten minutes after he'd left the house that night of the birthday party, we heard some popping sounds like firecrackers outside, or .22s, perhaps. There was a whoosh sound before the popping, so I figured someone was probably shooting off sky rockets. The popping sounds were too close together to be gunshots--so I had an idea who was shooting off the sky rockets. It was Pop. He was very high at the time, flying thirty thousand feet off of the ground.

Five minutes later, Pop came in from outside.

"Did you hear anything out there?" I asked him.

"No," he said, smiling and looking at me, his eyes spark-ling. "I didn't hear anything."

"It sounded like somebody was shooting off sky rockets out there."

"Naw," he said. "You know me," he said. "I wouldn't do that. It's against the law to shoot off fireworks in Playa Grande."

"Yeah, I know, it's illegal, so you wouldn't do that," I said, "for sure."

95

He smiled again and walked into the kitchen, where he got a beer and then came back and stood in the living room, his eyes sparkling with light.

The road to La Paz was only one lane south and one north, and it wound through the desert and the yellow hills toward La Paz, and the semi trucks heading north shook the van when they rushed past us as we listened to some Sonny Rollins.

"Pop was in the loony bin once, wasn't he?" Pete said.

"Yeah, he was," I said. "I was just a little kid when he went in there."

The judge that he had gone before that time, for taking the loaded Winchester into the cafe, didn't think it was a good idea for him to have so many rifles and pistols, and my father's lawyer made it clear at the hearing, I was later told, that my father had been diagnosed as manic depressive by a local psychiatrist, so instead of jail time my father was sent to the mental hospital in Camarillo. Many years after that, my father told me that Charlie "Bird" Parker was in Camarillo while he was there. He told me later that he'd seen a guy that was probably him a couple of times, and that sometimes, in the afternoon, he'd heard him playing jazz on a saxophone, the music drifting out through those big, old eucalyptus trees that rustled in the wind. So my father listened to Charlie "Bird" Parker play his saxophone. And we waited for my father to come back down to earth from the Pleiades.

After he had a couple of months of treatments, the doctors let him have visitors at the hospital, so my mother loaded my brother and me in the car and headed north in the old, blue Buick. The road went through Santa Monica and Malibu, then along the coast to Camarillo. As my mother turned and rocked the old Buick down the road, I would always get woozy and then carsick, so my mother always brought some lemon drops, which she would give to me to suck on so I wouldn't puke in the backseat. Art cried on and off and jumped from the front seat to the backseat, then back again, the whole trip. It took us about two hours to get to the hospital, and half-way through, we usually stopped to get something to drink at a hamburger stand that she found on the coast.

The hospital was a one-story group of Spanish-style buildings with red Spanish tiles on the roofs, all of the buildings painted white with brown trim on the window frames, so that it almost looked like a Spanish mission when you first saw it. Tall royal palms and eighty-foot tall eucalyptus trees stood out in front of the place and along the walkways toward the front door. Their big shadows fell across the green, manicured lawn.

When we got there, my mother parked and we walked through the front doors into the building, where there was a big, dark-skinned woman in a white dress sitting at a reception desk.

"We're here to visit Sabas Catalpa," my mother said.

The woman looked down at the papers in front of her, then thumbed through some cards in a file on her desk.

"Yes, he's here," she said. "Are you a relative?"

"I'm his wife," my mother said.

"The doctor would like to see you, before you visit your husband today," she said. "His office is the last door on the right, down this hallway." She stood up and pointed down the hall to her left.

My mother thanked her, and we walked down the hall to where four chairs were out in front of an office with a fogged glass door.

"I'm going to talk to the doctor," our mother said, "so you two need to be quiet. Do you understand? I don't want to leave you sitting out here."

We both nodded our heads and said that we would. Then she knocked on the glass of the door, and a voice from inside said, "Please come in," and all three of us went in.

The doctor said good morning, then smiled and stood up and held out his hand and introduced himself. He had glasses shaped like stop signs, and his hair was parted in the middle like T. S. Eliot.

"Please take a seat," the doctor said.

She sat down, and my brother and I stood to her right.

"How are you and your sons today?" he said.

"I'm worried about seeing my husband," Mom said. "Last time I saw him, he was really mean and angry, and he blamed me for putting him in here. I told him that it was either here or jail, but he didn't believe me."

"You can rest easy today, Mrs. Catalpa," he said. "Your husband is calmer today then he was before. He's doing very well."

"Is he still angry at me?" my mother said.

"No, he'll be different today," he said and leaned back in his chair. "He's been going through a series of shock therapy treatments for the past months, and he's responding well."

"Do the shock treatments hurt him at all?" she asked.

"No, it doesn't hurt him, even though the convulsions make it look as if they do," he said. "A patient has convulsions when the shocks are administered and then is unconscious for a few minutes. So it looks worse than it really is. And the good part is, it works."

"Could it hurt him?" she asked.

"Not really. He has responded as I thought he would, and he came through it just fine," he said. "He's young and strong. He's gone through several treatments now, and it has ended in the kind of results we hoped for."

"Is he still like himself, like the Sabas that we know?" she said.

"You'll find that he's very calm," he said. "He's a bit distant, but that will change down the line."

"That's good," my mother said. "I don't want him to be mad at me like he was before."

"He won't be mad today," the doctor said.

Mom thanked him, and we walked down the hall and

98

through a door with chicken-wire glass, into where people were waiting for visitors in a room full of couches and easy chairs. Pop was sitting near the window, looking out across the lawn and the bean fields beyond the trees. When we came in, he turned and looked at us, then back outside.

"Hi, honey," my mother said, "how are you doing?"

He looked at her as if he didn't see her, and then he said, "I'm okay," and looked out the window again. "My head's kind of smoggy, but I'm okay."

"I brought the kids to see you," she said and pulled us around and patted us on the head, as if she was counting to see if we were both there. "The doctor says you're doing well today," she said.

"That's good," he said. "I glad someone knows how I'm doing. I don't really know how I feel at the moment."

"You're losing weight," she said. "Is the food any good?"

"It's okay," he said. "It keeps me alive." He kept looking out the window, across the grass and through the trees, as if he had lost something out there, which he probably had.

A short, square-shouldered Mexican soldier with dark skin held up his hand as we approached him on the highway. Thirty feet behind him, there were more soldiers who looked just like the soldier near us. I knew that they were probably Yaquis.

"Momentito," the soldier said, as he looked into the van at us.

Many young Yaquis joined the Mexican army, generation after generation. The parents of the boys prepared them for joining. There were six soldiers camped on the roadside, two green tents and a bonfire. It was twilight, and one soldier started lighting coffee cans full of kerosene on fire. I could smell it on the wind. They were supposed signal that people were required to stop and be questioned and inspected. Another short soldier, this one in a starched uniform with a gold bar on his shoulder, stood questioning a tall, drunken man who'd probably gotten out of the old pickup parked just ahead of us at the side of the road. The lieutenant looked over at us, then back at the drunk. He said something to the drunken man, and the drunk got into the pickup and drove it over to the side of the tent, got out again, and sat down on the ground beside his pickup truck. The lieutenant walked over to my window, and I rolled it down. The other man stepped back and gave him room.

"Buenos dias, señor," he said. "Que tiene hoy? Tiene armas?" He looked me in the eyes.

"No armas aqui," I said.

"Tiene drogas?" he said.

"No, no tengo drogas," I said.

He studied my eyes without blinking his. "A donde van?"

"A La Paz," I said.

The same questions as before. All of these guys were very worried about drugs and arms.

He looked at Pete and then at me again.

"Gracias. Vayan, por favor," he said as he waved us through. At least this guy was polite.

The drunken man stood up, and a soldier next to him pushed him back down on the ground as we drove ahead, very slowly, safe and sane. As we drove down the road, I saw the drunk trying to get up again and the lieutenant pushing him down again, then doing it over again, and I remembered the big, drunken guy that my father had wrestled with forty years ago. That night, Pop had been ready to close the shop when the redheaded taxi driver came into the flower shop with the big, drunken guy. I was ten years old, at the time. Pop had been out of the hospital for five or six years, and he had been working hard in the shop and staying out of trouble. The big, drunken guy handed some money to the taxi driver near the door, and then the drunk staggered in and sat down in a chair in front of the desk that was there for people to write cards. The taxi cab driver walked over to the counter near the cash register with the money in his hand. I sat behind the counter, waiting for Pop to finish and close so we could all go out to eat. I was ten years old at the time. My mother and my brother were upstairs, in the house, getting ready to go to a little Mexican restaurant called The Acapulco Cafe.

"This guy wants a dozen roses," the taxi driver said.

"Does he want them in an arrangement or a box?" Pop said.

"How much are they in a box?" he said.

"Ten dollars in a box, fifteen in a vase," Pop said.

"OK. Give me a box," the taxi driver said and handed Pop a hundred dollar bill. "Here, take the money now, and give me the change. He's a little drunk."

"I can see that," Pop said, then went to the register, opened it and put the hundred in, got the change, and gave it to the cab driver. "I took out the tax," Pop said.

The cabbie put the money in his shirt pocket.

All of the roses were in a refrigerator with glass windows to display the flowers. The barbell that my father had made for himself out of a drive shaft and two lead weights sat in front of the glass window of the refrigerator. My father got the roses out of the refrigerator, cleaned them of their thorns, then got a gold box and put the roses in it on top of some wax paper and some fern. He tied a gold string around the box and handed it to the cabbie.

The big guy got up and staggered around the shop, looking at plants and flowers as he wove back and forth. His shoulders were four feet across, and his ears looked as if they'd been smashed a thousand times.

"You're not thinking about cheating this guy out of any money, are you?" Pop said. "He looks like a guy you don't want to piss off."

"Don't worry your little head about it," the cabbie said.

"I'm not worried about it at all, wiseass," my father said, "unless he comes over here to ask me for the change that you didn't give him."

The cab driver took the change and the gold box of roses and went over to the big guy and handed him the box. Then they talked for a while, and the big guy staggered out to the taxi and put the roses on the backseat, then he walked over to the cabbie and held out his hand. It looked as if he wanted his change, as predicted. The big guy had a flat nose, and he was in good shape except for his being drunk and staggering. The cabbie and the big guy talked for a minute outside the door, then the big guy came back into the shop with the cabbie behind him, and the big guy leaned on the counter and made it creak, his eyes red and bloodshot. The cabbie was pacing back and forth behind him.

"How much were those roses?" the big guy said.

"Ten dollars," Pop said, "plus the tax."

The big guy turned around and said, "You cheating son of a bitch."

He staggered over to the cabbie and knocked the guy's hat off of his head, and then grabbed his red hair and swung him around the shop a couple of times, and in doing that, he ripped out a V of the cabbie's hair, and the cabbie stumbled and fell into a bunch of chrysanthemums in big vases there on the floor, and the big guy took a swing at the cabbie and missed and knocked down eight or ten plants as he went after him.

The big guy looked back over his shoulder at the cabbie. "You skinny son of a bitch," he said. "I'm gonna kill you."

Pop came at the big guy from behind, pushed him down onto the floor, pulled the big guy's tan plaid sport coat over his head, and sat on his back, there on the cement floor, while the big guy wiggled around with my father on his back as if he was a bull rider in a rodeo.

"Quit moving, god damn it," Pop said, "or I'll bash your face in some more."

The taxi driver came after the guy on the ground and kicked him in the ribs, and the big guy moaned like a wounded bear.

"Cut that shit out, or I'll let him up," my father said.

The big guy tried to get up again, so my father pushed his face down onto the cement.

"Tell your mom to call the cops before this joker kills somebody," Pop said.

I ran upstairs and told my mother to call the cops, and then I went back downstairs, and after ten long minutes, the cops came, a black guy named Duke and a Mexican guy named Frank, both of them big, both of them destined to be future customers.

"You'd better grab onto this guy when I let him up," Pop said. "He's strong as hell." When the big guy moved, my father bashed his face against the cement floor again. Some blood on the cement shone in the light.

"Just let him up," Frank said. "I'll take care of him."

"It's your funeral," Pop said. He let go of the coat and stood behind the guy, Frank and Duke on either side of him. The big guy's back came up like a whale surfacing, and then he started swinging, and Frank grabbed his right arm and grabbed him around the neck and pulled his neck over his shoulder, and the big guy just went limp as spaghetti and passed out. Duke grabbed the big man's arms and put the handcuffs on his wrists behind his back while he was still on the ground.

"How'd you knock him out so quick?" Pop said.

"That's my special sleeper hold," Frank said and smiled. "I'm very good at it, aren't I? You did a good job yourself."

"Thanks," Pop said. "I was very lucky."

"Probably so," Frank said. "This guy's Godzilla."

The two cops cuffed the big guy and picked him up and carried him to the patrol car, where they put him in the backseat and closed the door.

Frank asked my father what had happened.

"The cabbie was trying to cheat the big guy out of ninety bucks," Pop said.

"Give me the money," Frank said to the cabbie, "unless you

want us to take you in."

The big guy was looking out the window now, yelling and struggling like a bull in a chute.

"I was going to give it to him later. Anyway, he owes me for the cab ride," the driver said.

"Right," Frank said. "You should have been a good boy."

The cab driver handed Frank the money.

"That big bastard said he was a sparring partner for Max Bear," the taxi driver said. "The big prick."

"I believe it," Frank said. "What were you thinking, trying to screw a guy like him out of money? You're lucky he didn't kill your skinny ass. And you're lucky we aren't taking you in."

His forehead where the hair had been ripped out was bleeding from every follicle. He looked at Frank and Duke and rubbed the bald V on his head. Then he went and got into his cab and drove off.

"You got your workout today," Frank said to Pop.

"That was enough exercise for a few days," Pop said.

There were a lot of reasons why my father had worked out with weights when he was young, besides fighting with drunks and seeing a muscle-building ad from Charles Atlas in a magazine. He'd been born with a club-foot, so he'd dragged that around for his first five years, since my grandmother hadn't had enough horse sense to put his ankle in a splint to straighten it up when he was a baby. Then, when he grew up in the Colony, where all of the Mexicans lived, he had surgery that straightened out his ankle. He had a deep, curved scar from his heel to the ball of his foot from that operation.

His Uncle Guillermo was six feet tall, and he always wore a small-brimmed, gray Stetson hat along with a tan suit, and he had a cigar in his mouth when he came to visit us at the shop. His face looked just like a picture of Geronimo that we had on our wall, so Art and I always called him Uncle Geronimo when we talked about him. He was the type of guy who would just bust into the bathroom, even if you were sitting on the pot, take a piss in the bathtub, and think nothing of it. Uncle Geronimo had run a fertilizer business in Mexico, and he had continued the business in California.

My father already had a bad limp, and then he had an accident while working for Uncle Geronimo, the chicken shit magnate. Pop had told me about one day when he had been loading chicken shit into the back of a flatbed truck. He stood ankle-deep in chicken shit, and it began to rain, and the ground and the chicken shit got wet and soggy. He shoveled the soon-to-be fertilizer up and into the back of the truck. He was at the foot of a hill, just down from the truck, and the emergency brake slipped and the truck rolled down off of a mound of chicken shit and right over Pop's bad leg. The ground was soggy and muddy, so he was pressed down into the chicken shit and mud, and that had probably saved his leg from being completely flattened and later amputated. He ended up in the County Hospital once again, with his leg in traction and a sand bag hanging there in front of him like a pendulum. His leg was broken in a dozen or more places, so he lay there in the hospital for two months. When he got out of there, his limp was even worse than before. Still, he had withstood all of that trouble, all of those accidents, and yet he couldn't do anything that would help him stay off the couch for months on end or keep from raving around the country with his guns during the other part of the year.

When Uncle Geronimo came to visit us, we could always smell his cigar before we saw him. He'd come up from the south illegally about thirty years before, with no entrance visa and no passport, just put three of his tan suits on, one over the other, and walked across the border, his Stetson hat on his head and his big cigar in his mouth. He must have looked like a big, rich, fat cattle baron from some ranch in Texas to the customs officer, so the guy asked him his citizenship, and Uncle just said, "U. S. A.," so the immigration guy let him into California, where he then stayed for the rest of his life, not counting the times he went down to Mexico to visit and then stroll, with a cigar in his mouth, back across the border into the States every time.

Pete and I rolled south down the road, the Sea of Cortez to the east of us, a blue ribbon of water beyond the yellow beach. I took a drink of water from my bottle and looked down the road and across the water toward the mainland, and I put some Coltrane on.

"Where do you want to stop?" Pete said.

"Mulege will be good," I said. "It's getting late."

15

In Mulege, it was almost dark, the white buildings glowing orange, the sun just at the top of the mountains to the west, long shadows lying across the streets. Rain started as I drove down the first street into town, and when we came to the zocalo, there was a thirty-foot high orange and blue tent standing on the beach across from the square. Above the doorway, there was a sign that read:

CIRCO VELASQUEZ
Alambristas, Payasos
Actos Peligrosos
Magico y Fantastico
y
Los Toltecas Muy Antiguas

Outside the tent stood two old, white horses, and toward the back of the tent, there was a mountain lion pacing back and forth in its cage.

"It looks like a pretty small circus," Pete said.

"It's probably a big deal for them to come to town," I said. "They don't get much entertainment around here."

Near the beach was a hotel, and beside it, there were palm-covered palapas for shade, cement slabs, and half-assed fire rings for people who camped or were in RVs. I stopped and went into the hotel, paid an old guy for two days, and parked the van next to a cement pallet.

We found a place to eat on the zocalo, and we ate some fish tacos and drank a couple of beers. As we sat there, the sun went down and the lights of the town came on. Rain began to fall heavily, splashing in the street and making the tent across the street look as if it was behind a gray curtain.

The circus started at seven, so we ran through the rain and bought a couple of tickets from a girl in the booth. Inside the tent, we went up into the bleachers. A fine mist fell from the ceiling of the tent. I looked around and saw that it was the rain being filtered through the nylon cloth of the tent. It looked as if they didn't expect to ever have rain in this desert, so their tent was a kind of sieve. All of the crowd, and all of the benches, and all of the chairs and equipment of the circus were wet and shone in the lights. It felt as if we were in a cold fog, the air wet with mist. Young men filled the bleachers to our right, and they hooted and howled like a bunch of Apache warriors doing a war dance. I figured they were all pretty close to being Apaches, even if they wouldn't admit it. For five hundred years, the Spaniards had told the whole population of Mestizos that they were Spanish. But my father always pointed at his cheekbones and said, "Here's my Indian blood." He hadn't been so easily convinced that being part Indian was a bad thing to be.

The crowd of half breeds and the two of us all sat in the descending mist while all of the boys hooted and hollered and waited for the Circo Velasquez to begin.

The first act was the knife thrower, a five-foot tall guy with a huge mustache who wore a Spanish conquistador's helmet, a breast plate with red fringe around his waist, and red-and-white checkered pants. With him was his assistant, a beautiful, dark-skinned woman with long black hair, who wore a black and gold, sequined outfit that showed off her legs and her figure. She had a big smile on her face. Two clowns came out on unicycles. One had a three-foot high, feathered headdress and a blue costume with yellow polka dots. The other clown wore a red conquistador helmet to match his red breastplate and costume, and he had a red beard that reached down to his waist. They both carried a couple of wooden swords that they kept juggling back and forth. They kept circling the knife thrower and the woman, chasing each other, the red clown blowing a penny whistle and swinging his wooden sword above him as if he was Cortez, Pizzaro, and Ponce De Leon, all squeezed together into one man.

The woman's gold sequins glistened in the lights. She moved to stand in front of a round piece of plywood that was painted like an Aztec calendar, yet all cut up and ragged from the thousands of past knives being thrown and stuck in it. She stood with her legs and arms spread wide, as if she wanted to embrace the knives that were to come, as the clowns pulled a cloth banner out above her with "La Castigation de la traidor Malinche" painted in red. Then the clowns started juggling the swords again. The crowd booed at the sight of the sign. I knew that Malinche was the traitor to the Aztecs, Cortez's mistress, and it looked as if the crowd knew about her, too. With a drum roll from the clown in the dunce cap, the knife thrower picked up a knife from a large pile, aimed with both eyes, and threw it. It flew through the air, then stuck with a thunk above the woman's head. And he threw another knife and another knife, until there were maybe thirty knives framing the Indian woman, the blades shining like rays of light around her and her sequins glistening. The clowns kept riding their unicycles around and around and between the knife-thrower and then dodging the knives as if they were only birds flying by. The woman stood still, framed by the shiny, silver knives. Finally, when he had finished throwing all of the knives that he had, he took off his helmet and bowed, and the Indian woman bowed as well, as the crowd hooted and hollered and applauded some more.

For their grand finale, the woman turned sideways, put a foot-long cigar in her mouth, struck a match and lit the cigar, and then stood there until the knife-thrower put on a black blindfold, turned around, and threw another knife that somehow stuck in the cigar and carried it back to stick in the plywood calendar behind her. The fog and the mist continued to come down from the top of the tent, while the rain came down heavily outside, sounding like thousands of little drums beating, and everything and everybody inside was wet, so the knife thrower wiped the rain from his face and the woman dripped water all around her as she grabbed the man's hand. Both of them bowed once, twice, and three times, as the crowd roared with praise, and then with a flourish and a flip of the conquistador's cape, they exited through a curtain, the crowd applauding for more.

The clowns began juggling six wooden swords back and forth across the single center ring. Then the head-dressed clown dropped the swords, picked up a trumpet, and played the tune that meant the cavalry was coming. A dark skinned Indian man wearing only a pair of black bun huggers came in to the center ring. His body and face and head were covered with tribal tattoos that were so thick they looked as if they were many-colored mold. He walked from the curtain to the metal chairs, then started piling the chairs one on top of the other, catching the chairs that the clowns threw up to him and doing handstands and flips on each chair, until they were eight chairs high, the descending mist making them all shine and sparkle in the light. The clowns went to stand on either side of the chairs, and they moved back and forth as if they were spotting him, which was far from the truth. The tattooed man climbed all of the way up to the top chair, where he stood on both hands, then on one hand, then pulled his legs over onto his shoulders and stood on both of his hands again, so that he looked like a tattooed ball with a head. After that he started dropping the chairs down to the clown with the helmet on his head to catch, until the tattooed man stood on his hands on the bottom chair and did a flip, then landed on his feet on the ground. There he bowed to the audience, which applauded and hooted and whistled as he exited. Just then, two drunken men who looked full-blooded Indian staggered out into the center ring and started fighting each other, swinging their arms and missing and falling down, then standing and falling down again. Then two clowns on their monocycles circled the two men three times then herded them back into the bleachers, got off of their unicycles and sat the two drunks down in the first row of the bleachers, where two men from the crowd grabbed the drunks and held them apart from each other.

Then the clowns went into the cage where the mountain lion paced back and forth. The clown with the white beard let his unicycle drop and then picked up a chair and a whip and started cracking the whip above the head of the mountain lion. The other clown continued to yell and shake and run around inside the cage, as if he was scared. The clown with the helmet cracked the whip and the mountain lion jumped up onto a stool, and the clown poked a chair at him, so that the mountain lion hissed his anger and pawed at the clown with its teeth bared. The door at the back of the cage opened again, and the red clown cracked the whip and the mountain lion ran out through a door that led out of the tent and behind a curtain. Finally, the clowns came out of the cage and stood bowing to the applause and the whistling of the audience.

The bearded clown grabbed a megaphone and walked into a spotlight in the center of the ring.

"La Alambrista," he announced through the megaphone, "is magnifico and she walks the wire like a bird, without a net."

The same young woman that had been with the knife-thrower came out from the back, the spotlight following her as she walked. She wore a black feather headdress and a black, sequined suit, and she grabbed a thick ribbon and climbed up, hand over hand, toward a platform, where a black wire led to a second platform on the other side of the tent. Through the descending mist, she looked as if she was behind a sheet of gauze, the lights from below casting her long shadow above her on the roof of the tent. Below her, the clowns picked up a big hoop covered with torn and tattered canvas that they held between them, and under the woman, as she walked from the ground to the top of a pole thirty feet high, her bare feet grasping the heavy cable. When she got to the top, she grabbed a long stick that lay on the platform and, with it, started walking across the black wire to the other side of the tent and the other platform.

The two drunks got up again and started swinging at each

other, but the clowns quickly herded them back into the bleachers where two sober men from earlier scolded them and sat them down again.

Below the tightrope walker were the dirt and the circus ring and the cage, no safety net, only the tattered, yellow canvas in the hoop that the clowns had returned to hold just beneath her, while they ran here and there in a dramatized frenzy. As she walked the high wire, her black hair swayed back and forth on her back. Then it seemed as if there was no wire, as if she was just walking through the air somehow, and I blinked my eyes and looked again and the wire had returned. When she'd walked half the span between the platforms, she stopped and raised her left knee to her chest and stood on her right foot for a moment. Then she crouched and sprung up to come down on two feet and proceed toward the end of the wire and the connecting platform. She reached the platform, and the Apaches in the audience roared and whistled and hooted and applauded, and as the rest of the audience gave her a standing ovation, the Aztec princess wrapped her legs around the thick black ribbon and slid down in slow motion to the ground. The clowns picked up the trumpet and the penny whistle and started tooting their ancient tune again. Then she bowed, waved, and smiled to the audience and ran out through a break in the red curtain.

"She is really a beautiful woman," I said.

"She's something all right," Pete said.

Then a dozen four-foot tall men poured out from behind the curtain. Each of them looked like some old Toltec statues of short, stout men that I'd seen in books and on museum shelves. My father had always said that he was part Toltec, since Toltecs had ruled Jalisco until the Aztecs had come along, and then the Spanish had shown up. The dwarves piled one on top of the other, making a pyramid in the middle of the red ring, then tumbled down to then make another pyramid that blossomed from the center of the pile like a rose. Some music came from the loudspeakers, a lot of flutes and a lot of horns tooting in the background, and the clown with the conquistador helmet on came out and circled the pyramid of Toltecs on his unicycle and started waving his sword in the air above him. The Toltecs' human pyramid tumbled, and the fifteen little men ran over and encircled the clown, then chased him around the ring a couple of times, and finally chased him out through the curtain, and they went out behind him.

With that, the spotlights came on bright in the tent, and the clown with the headdress and the flute bowed to the audience and said, "Gracias. Gracias," and bowed to the audience and then bowed again. Just then, the two drunks started swinging at each other in the bleachers again, since their custodians had left them alone. Everyone stood and began to file out of the tent, leaving the two drunks to fight as much as they felt like, fighting in the center of the ring. We all moved toward the doorway in the canvas that we had all come in through. The rain outside was still coming down hard, splashing in the puddles that surrounded the tent.

"What was that all about?" Pete said.

"It looked like the conquistadors against the Indians," I said. "The Indians seemed to come out on top in this version."

I wanted to go to the trailers behind the big tent and find the beautiful Indian woman who had walked the wire. I wanted to see her up close, but I didn't say anything to Pete. We just walked through the puddles. And I thought, Maybe I'll see her again somewhere, if I'm lucky.

There was an old, beat up trailer with a painting on the side of a blue eye surrounded by eagle feathers. On each side of the eye were six lines, six broken lines on the left, six solid on the right. And below the eye and the lines, it read:

don Diego, El Indio
con
Dos Cientos Años
Memorias del Futuro

"We have to see this," I said. "How often do you meet a

two-hundred-year-old Indian?"

I opened the trailer's door and stepped inside out of the rain, Pete following close behind me. We had gotten soaked just standing outside for two minutes, so we stood in the trailer, dripping onto the floor. When we closed the door, it was dark inside except for a dim, blue light toward the end of the trailer that lit the face of an old man who was sitting with his legs crossed on the seat of a chair. His face was as wrinkled and lined as a topographical map of the Copper Canyon. To his right, there was a table and two more chairs. He was smoking a pipe that dipped down six inches below his chin. Its smoke was blue, along with us and everything else inside, from a blue light behind the old man.

"Welcome caballeros," the old man said.

The smoke rose from his pipe into the small trailer.

"Don Diego?" I said.

"Yes," he said, "that's what they call me today."

"We need some help," I said. "We're trying to find someone."

"Sit down," he said. "Make yourselves comfortable. This will take a while."

We sat down in cowhide-covered chairs, the hair still on them.

"I'll count the yarrow sticks for you," he said. "You can ask any question that you want for seventy pesos."

"I only get one question?" I said.

"You can ask as many question as you want," he said. "But each time I move and count the yarrow sticks it will cost you seventy pesos."

He held out his palm and smiled and showed his perfect white teeth. His wrinkles folded and unfolded on his face like a hundred arroyos.

"Here's the seventy pesos," I said, putting the bills on the table. The rain came down hard outside, pounding on the roof of the trailer. What could a little fortune telling hurt? I thought.

114

Anyway, it was a good idea to wait until the rain let up to go back to the van, or to retire to some cantina that sold cold beer and good tequila nearby, where we could sit for a while and stay dry out of the rain.

"How do we do this?" I said.

"Please," he said, "think only of your question."

"Sure," I said. And I thought, How are we going to catch up to Pop and take him back home? What is he after? What in the hell am I doing down here? Three questions, but he'd never know the difference, I thought.

He waved a handful of foot-long sticks the diameter of match sticks in the air above him, set half of them to his right and the rest to his left, then placed one stick between the first two fingers of his left hand. He started pushing away the sticks to the left four at a time, putting more sticks between his fingers all along.

"Do you want to know my question?" I said.

"No, thank you," he said. "It's none of my damn business. Concentrate on your question, while I move the sticks to find the lines for you."

He swept the seventy pesos up, put it in it in a small, leather pouch that he wore on a string around his neck, and then picked up a thick, yellow book that sat on the table in front of him.

"What is that book?" I asked.

"It's a very old book, 'The I Ching,' an excellent translation," he said. "First edition."

"'The I Ching'?" I said.

"That's right," he said. "You know about this book, I see. It's the best divining book that you can find. Tested by centuries."

He closed his eyes, then quickly shifted the pile of sticks back and forth, drawing one line, then another, and another, while he shifted the long sticks from his right hand to his left, stuck more sticks between the fingers of his left hand, drew a solid line, then a broken one, and then started again and did the same, moving the sticks from the piles back and forth and drawing lines all along, until he had drawn six lines on the pad in front of him.

"Wait a minute. Can't anybody do 'The I Ching,' if they have the book?" I said.

"Yes, but I am really good at it, and I am colorful and entertaining, so I can do it much better than most can. Besides, I've had many years of practice and I'm as old as the mountains, which counts for something."

"Okay, what do you have there?" I looked at the notebook. Four of the lines were solid, two broken.

He opened the book then read aloud to us.

"'Forty-nine. Revolution, Leather, Skin,'" he said. "'In revolution, the sun of the self is truth. This is creative, developmental, fruitful, and perfect. All regret vanishes.'" He puffed on his pipe and blew out a thin stream of smoke. "'Wrapped up in yellow ox-hide,'" he said, "'the sun of the self is the good fortune of expedition in revolution: no blame. It is not auspicious to go on an expedition; even if correct, there is danger. Revolutionizing words formulated thrice, there is certainty. Regret vanishes. With sincerity one changes destiny for the better. Yang. A great person changes like a tiger. There is certainty without divination. Superior people transform. Inferior people change on the surface. To go on an expedition is unlucky, to remain correct is auspicious.'

"'This hexagram symbolizes fire rising from a marshy lake.

116

The Superior Man regulates the calendar and thus ensures that men are clear about times and seasons.'

"The bottom line: 'For strength, use yellow ox hide. Such aids to strength are necessary, for this line cannot suit itself to its position.'

"The second line: 'On the day the revolution is completed, to advance brings good fortune and is free from error. This line presages great blessings.'

"The third line: 'To advance now would bring misfortune and persistence would lead to further troubles. When talk of revolution has thrice arisen, then act with confidence. What else could you do under the circumstances?'"

As he spoke, I kept thinking about the beautiful Aztec tight-rope walker. Don't let your wanger be your guide, for once, I said to myself. Concentrate.

"We have to go on, whether it's promising or not," I said.

"They are your questions, so you are the only one that can answer them," he said.

"Isn't that the way it always is?" I said.

"Of course," he said. "How else should it be? There is no magic here, just your unconscious mind helping you along."

"That's all right. I don't want to deal with magic anyway . . . When did you start using the book?" I said.

"Many, many years ago, I got my first copy in China on the Silk Road, way back. Met a poet in a tavern there and he gave it to me. Then an Austrian psychiatrist whom I met in Europe suggested that I take a good look at it again, so that I could be more successful in reading people's fortunes. So I've been using it ever since. Trust me, it's the best book that you can get of its kind for your money." He puffed on his pipe some more. "I've seen a lot of people and a lot of things."

The air was thick with blue smoke by then. He reached down to the floor and grabbed a bottle of tequila and a glass, poured the glass half full, and took a sip.

"The fourth line: 'Regret vanishes and confidence is established. A change of government brings good fortune. Good fortune in the sense that people will put their faith in your objective.'

"The fifth line: 'The great man accomplishes change like a tiger; he is so confident that he does not need to employ divination. His accomplishing the change 'like a tiger' means in a brilliantly civilized manner.'

"The sixth line: 'The superior man brings about the change like a leopard, and lesser men promptly switch their allegiance. To advance now brings misfortune. Righteous persistence brings good fortune to those who remain where they are.' The superior man brings out the change, and 'like a leopard' means that he does so in a manner that is exceedingly graceful. That lesser men 'promptly switch their allegiance' means that they readily accept his lead."

He sat back in his chair, lit his pipe again, puffed a few times, then smiled. "No moving lines," he said. "And so . . . that's all that the oracle has to say for now, caballeros. Do you have any questions?"

"Maybe," I said.

It sounded as if there were a few storms ahead. But there was no choice. We had to go on, no matter what this old Indian said was good or bad.

"So we'll try to go ahead 'like a leopard,' carefully, as you said. Where are you from, anyway?"

"I'm from all over. My ancestors were travelers, just as I am. Mostly Yaqui and Tarahumara. But I'm like your father, a force of nature, part of all and a member of none."

"All right," I said. 'Revolution,' I thought. 'Fire rising from a lake.' How should we proceed? Be cautious. Go ahead. Of course. There was no other choice for us anyway. 'Like a leopard' stalking its prey we would head south. Then I thought, He said "like your father"?

"You've met my father?"

"I think so," he said. "He looks a lot like you. The same nose. And his eyes are like this young man's eyes, ice blue."

"Where did you see him?"

"That was in Santa Rosalia, two weeks ago."

"Did he say where he was going?"

"Just that he was going south. He was interested in horses and in some land in Jalisco."

"Anything else?"

"He knows that you are looking for him. Nothing more." He puffed on his pipe. "I think that we're finished, my friends, unless you want to take another swim in the river, for seventy pesos again."

"No, that will be fine," I said. "I guess that's all."

"All right. So now it's time for a little more tequila, then a siesta," Don Diego said, and a smile broke through his wrinkled face.

16

In Magdalena Bay, Pete and I went to a beach where a six pongas had been pulled out on the sand, their white hulls patched with unpainted fiber glass, and we asked around about the old man, if they'd seen him, if perhaps he'd come there. We'd been asking people all along the road about him, showing his picture and telling them what was like, but everyone had said that they hadn't seen a man like that. One old guy had told us to ask the fishermen further down on the beach, so we walked toward two men who stood beside what seemed to be their long red and blue ponga, with an old and battered 75-horse engine screwed to its transom. One man had a blue Dodgers hat on and the other a black Yankees hat. They looked at us when we walked up, and both said buenos tardes.

I smiled and said the same, then described my father and asked them if they'd seen a man like him who wore a black Stetson.

"There was a man like that nine or ten days ago, I think," the Yankees man said. "But he wore a different kind of hat."

"No, six days ago," the Dodgers man said.

"I think that it was maybe two weeks ago. That was when we caught our little marlin," the Yankees man said.

"Maybe so," the Dodgers man said. "This man was a little bit like a gringo, but he spoke Spanish like a Mexican. Maybe he was Cubano?"

"He had blue eyes," the Yankees man said, "but he wore a leather hat that covered his ears, like the old pilots used to wear. He wanted to go fishing for marlin. We gave him a price and he said that he would come back soon and go out. He wanted to catch a big fish, like his father had done, he told us. He said that he was coming back, in a couple of days."

"So when was this?" I said.

"I think it was probably two weeks ago," the Yankees man said.

"No, I think it was only nine days ago," the Dodgers man said.

"He had blue eyes like a gringo, or a Spaniard, that man. We've been waiting for him, but I don't think that he's coming back."

"He was probably a Cubano," the Yankees man said.

"I don't know if he's coming back or not," the Dodgers man said. "It would be good if he came because the business of fishing is terrible. We need somebody to go out with us so that we can make a few pesos."

"What did he say?" I said. "Did he say where he was going?"

"Maybe," the Dodgers man said, "I can't remember what he said very well. We drank a lot of tequila in the cantina with this man with the pilot hat." He took off his hat and fanned himself.

They both had black grease on his hands, and their t-shirts were wet with sweat.

"That man wasn't a Cubano," the Dodgers man said.

"Who knows? But I think that he was a pilot," the Dodgers man said.

"What kind of pilot wears a hat like that when he is driving a car through the desert?" the Yankees man said.

"Maybe he was a pilot from a long time ago?" the Dodgers man said.

"Maybe so," the Yankees man said. "Maybe you and the boy want to go fishing for a big fish? We have a very good price, and I think that now we know where the big fish are, since we saw one jumping for us just yesterday."

"No, not today," I said. "We have to go south after my father."

"We do not see big fish jumping every day," the Yankees man said. "I thought that the pilot would come back, but now I don't think so."

"Maybe not, but I'm waiting," the Dodgers man said.

"If you see my father some place," the Yankees man said, "tell him to go to hell for me."

"I'll do that," I said.

17

In La Paz we got a room at an old hotel in the center of town, near the zocalo, then went out to eat and drink. There was a strip club called Club Papeete that Pop had mentioned on a postcard that he'd sent Art two months before.

Art,
  I'm with the beautiful women of Club Papeete. All of them are wahines from Paradise. I am Paul Gauguin in Tahiti among the natives. I am Joaquín in love with Rosita. I will take them all to Disneyland and Universal City.
  Don't tell your mother.
  I wonder, Who is the Cisco Kid?
        Sabas Joaquín Gauguin, your Pop

I remembered one day when he had ten thousand dollars in his pocket on a Friday afternoon. He left driving toward who knows where.

"I'll be back in a minute," he said to me and my mother.

Then she called me up and said, "He's on a spree again, buying everything. Please come over here so that you can talk some sense into him when he comes back this time. I think he went to the bank."

So I'd gone over to the house, and just as I got there he drove up in the Ram Charger and revved the engine a couple of times and smiled at us through the window. He got out and opened the hood on the Ram.

"How much money did you get at the bank?" my mother said as she stood there with her arms folded, her face white with fear.

"Just ten thousand," he said.

"Ten thousand? That's a lot of money. Where you going now?" my mother said.

"There are some things that I need to buy. Bargains," he said.

"Like what?" she said.

"Don't worry about it."

"Of course not. 'Don't worry about it.' Last week you took off and came back with an old, beat up Mustang," she said.

"Hell," he said, "that was a steal. It's a great car."

"Pop, it's an old wreck," I said.

"Naw, it just needs a little body work and it will be perfect. The engine's fantastic."

"No more cars," my mother said.

He just smiled, got in the Ram, and peeled rubber down the road. I waited around, talking to my mother. "He'll be all right," I said. "Don't worry about him."

"Sure, he'll be all right. Last week he spent nine thousand dollars on cars and trailers. Now he has ten thousand more that he wants to spend on some other wreck."

We went inside, and my mom made me a sandwich. At four that Sunday afternoon, he drove up in a silver Mercedes sedan.

"Beautiful, isn't it," he said. "I saw it and I couldn't get it off my mind. So I made the guy an offer, and he took it. A deal."

"Where are you going to park it? The street's full of your cars already," I said.

"Oh, that's easy to fix. I'll rent some garages. That way they'll be perfect. Out of the sun," he said.

"I told you no more cars," my mother said. "You already have five cars. How many do you need?"

"Hell, this Mercedes was a steal," he said.

"Everything's a steal," I said.

"No, not everything, but a lot of things. I can sell this

124

Mercedes and make money on it."

"When are you going to sell it?" I asked.

"I'll sell it pretty soon."

"You've had that trailer for two years and you haven't used it once, and you just keep saying 'I'm going to sell it,'" my mother said.

"I thought that you were going to sell the Mustang," I said.

"I'll sell it when I get the body work done," he said.

"Sure thing," my mother said. "In a year or two. Look, you have a Mustang that needs body work, a Mercedes that needs who-knows-what, a Winnebago with a flat spare tire on the back, a huge Ford Van, a Ram Charger, an Airstream trailer, and a Citroen that doesn't run and is just sitting in the backyard. When are you going to get rid of some of these?"

I stayed out of it, just standing there and smoking a cigarette. He took off again in the Mercedes, peeling rubber, on his way to add something else to his car collection.

Now it looked as if he was collecting a bunch of women from a place called Club Papeete. So we found the place, right on the main street of town. We had to see what damage he had done.

The outside walls of the strip joint had a big painting of women wearing only lava-lava skirts. It was supposed to look like Tahiti or some other South Seas island along with what looked like a blue statue of some Polynesian god and a couple of yellow and brown men standing and sitting in the jungle. ¿De donde lluegamos? ¿Por que estamos aqui? ¿A donde vamos? was painted in the top left corner. Whoever had painted the mural had seen some paintings by Gauguin and given it a try, and they were pretty good, in a primitive way. Above the door was a red neon sign.

Club Papeete, Live Nude Girls

We paid a three-hundred pound doorman ten bucks each and went in. It was dark inside except for a round stage in the center of the room, where a skinny, dark skinned girl danced naked except for her black cowboy hat and her black high heels. She danced and squirmed like a mascara snake to the song "Norwegian Wood." We sat down at a table next to the stage. When my eyes adjusted to the dark, I saw that there were nine other women sitting in two booths on the other side of the stage. Two of them came over to our table and sat down, a blonde next to me and a brunette next to Pete. The blonde wore a black, sequined dress cut down to her navel in front. A bare-breasted waitress in a short lava-lava and high heels walked over, tray in hand.

We ordered two Bohemias.

"I'm glad the girls are 'live,'" I said to Pete.

"Yeah, it's better that way," he said and laughed.

"You buy me one cognac?" the blonde girl clasping my right arm said, putting her face close to mine so that I could smell her ten-peso perfume.

The girl beside Pete also asked him to buy her a drink, also cognac, of course. I knew that the women in these places always ordered something expensive, or at least a customer would pay for something expensive. That didn't mean that they'd really been given what they ordered. Yet it didn't make a lot of difference, since we weren't the ones doing their drinking.

"Sure, bring them what they want," I said. "Por favor."

When our beers and their drinks came, the women sipped the little snifters as if it was really cognac, then put the glasses on the table. I knew that it was tea in their glasses, or watered down coke, or kool aid. This was the way these places had to make as much money as they could off of their horny patrons as fast as they could, while they had their teeth in them.

"You like me?" the blonde said as she reached over and rested her hand on my crotch.

"You're nice and shy, aren't you?" I said.

"You want me?" she said.

"I want to ask you something," I said.

126

She took my right hand and put it on her breast, then straddled my leg and started undulating her hips on my thigh.

"You like to fuck with me?" she said.

"On any other day, I would like to fuck with you, but not today," I said. "I just want to ask if you saw this man." I took the photo of Pop out of my pocket and showed it to her in the dim, red light.

"Dos ciento dollares," she said. "You fuck with me."

"Look, how about twenty dollars and you just take a look at the photo," I said. I showed her a twenty-dollar bill and held up the picture.

"Dos ciento dollares for fucking or for talking," she said. "I think you one chip gringo."

She frowned, glanced at the photo, put down her full glass of kool aid, then got up and walked back to the other side of the stage to sit and lurk like a raccoon with the other women who waited there in two booths. The wall behind them was an island scene painted in day glow paint, and it glowed blue and green and red in the black light. The brunette with Pete stood up and pulled him up beside her, then pulled him toward the back of the bar and into a dark hallway.

"Hey," I hollered. "Where in the hell are you going?"

Pete looked back at me and shrugged, then slipped into the hallway behind the brunette. They disappeared in the dark.

"Wonderful," I said.

I figured he was twenty, old enough to take care of himself, or else I hoped he was, so I let it go. I'd just wait for him. I thought, Don't stick your nose in your son's sex life, even if it involves a full-fledged hooker in a Mexican bar. I sipped my beer, watched the stripper on stage, and looked at the ten customers in the place. They were all being attacked by the girls, all being asked the same questions that the girls asked everyone they saw. Three men in suits stood in the back of the room, in the shadows, and watched what was going on in the bar. They were silhouetted by red light, and it looked as if they stood in a fire.

I waited for Pete for fifteen minutes, twenty minutes. The whores stayed in their booths. No one came to my table except the waitress, who brought me a second Bohemia.

After half an hour and two nude dancers, I started to worry about him. Why in the hell had I let him go with that girl in the first place? You're a father, I thought. Have some sense and go and get him. He could be dead back there.

I got up and walked to the hallway where they had gone. There was just a dim, yellow light bulb at the end of the hall. I walked back to a door on the left, tapped on it, and waited. No one came to the door. I tried the handle and it was open, so I opened the door, then looked into a room filled with blue light. No one was in the room. There were three other closed doors along one wall. I went over and tapped on the first door. No one answered. I tried the doorknob, opened the door, and looked into a musty-smelling room with an unmade bed against the wall. Then I tapped on the second door. No answer again. The door was locked.

"Pete," I said, "you in there?"

"Just a minute," Pete said from inside.

After a very long minute the door opened and Pete came out with the girl, his arm on her shoulder. At least he was alive. The girl smiled at me.

"What's the problem?" he said.

"We aren't here for this," I said. "This place is dangerous. I thought that I lost you."

"She says that she loves me," he said.

"Did you pay her?"

"Just a hundred bucks. That's all that I had . . . It's weird, but I think I love her, too," he said. "Maybe we can come back here later and I can get to know her better. Maybe meet her family. Maybe we can save all of these girls from being whores, you know. Get a few big guys and come back and get them."

"What are you talking about?" I said. "Come on, let's get back on the track. You sound like your grandfather. It would be wonderful to save all of the whores from a seedy life, but we can't. No one can. You had me worried."

"I thought that she might know something about Grandpa."

"Sure. And does she?"

"She says that she's seen a few old guys around here, but no one that looked like Grandpa. Look, we were talking, and we were just getting ready to get into the good part. Can you give me another hundred bucks?"

"You're kidding?" I said. "I'm not giving you any more money to give her."

"But she promised that she's going to give me a free lap dance, then the rest. I think she really loves me."

"Cut it out, for Christ's sake. Nothing's free around here," I said. "She just loves your dinero. Let's get the hell out of here, before we end up getting killed."

"But she's really a nice girl."

"You can fall in love some other time."

"She's really intelligent. She has a master's degree in ceramics, and she has four kids, a sick mother, and a sick sister to feed at home."

"Sure," I said.

"Her name's Rosa. You'd like her if you talked to her."

"You're the most gullible person in North America."

The three-hundred pound bouncer came down the hall and stood staring at me, then gestured with his hand for me to get back into the bar.

"OK, I'm going," I said. The bouncer's bald head shone in the yellow light.

I went back down the hallway, into the bar, and to our table, and the bouncer followed me. Let him get his money's worth and maybe he'll keep his head screwed on, I thought. What else can I do?

The three-hundred pound bouncer lumbered back to the front door, where he stopped and folded his arms.

Fifteen minutes later, Pete and Rosa walked out of the hallway and back to our table and sat down.

"Welcome back," I said.

She leaned over and spoke into my right ear. "You give me one hundred dollars more, yes?"

"He already gave a hundred, and now you want another hundred? I thought that you loved him?"

"He only pays for dancing," she said. "I give him one extra good time. He say you have more money for me."

"Since you love him, how about leaving it at one hundred dollars?" I said.

"Oh, you like deal. Okay," she said. "Eduardo puede talk with you." She grabbed the twenty and joined the other raccoons in the dark booths framed by day glow palm and banana trees.

"Free?" I said to Pete. "She's the most expensive free whore I ever met. I hope the suits don't give us any trouble."

"You just bring out her bad side. She's really great," he said. "I really do think that I love her."

"We don't have time to fuck around right now. We have to try and get out of here alive without giving her any more money."

"She just has to take care of her family. So maybe I should give her the other hundred," he said.

"Maybe so," I said. "The only problem is that you don't have another hundred dollars to give her."

"I guess that a guy could get in a lot of trouble in a place like this," Pete said.

"You guess?" I said. "We are in a lot of trouble."

On stage, a new dancer came out covered in long feathers that flowed across her delicious body like little rivers. As she danced, she dropped her clothes and feathers onto the stage. Then she did the splits and turned and crawled like a leopard across the floor toward our table. It was the old standard leopard crawl, but it was well done. Then I recognized her. Or I thought

130

that I did. It was the beautiful Indian woman from the circus, the tightrope walker who dodged knives in her spare time. How in the hell did she get down here?

She smiled and stood and went back to swing on the brass pole like a kid on a merry-go-round, except that she was naked with a few long feathers in her hair.

"She's the girl from the circus," I said, "isn't she?"

"If it's her, she's a fast mover," Pete said. "How could she do that?"

"Don't ask me. All I know is that it's either her or her twin sister."

"Maybe so," he said. "Why'd you give the other one that money?" he said.

"That was just to get her to talk to me. Anyway, she said that she wants two hundred bucks for whatever she does, even if it is just to talk. It's expensive information they have around here."

The Indian girl finished her dance, picked up the feathers from the stage, and headed toward the back.

I got up and went after her. "Hey," I yelled. "Momentito."

She turned and looked at me, and then I felt a big hand on my shoulder and looked back at the giant, bald bouncer again.

"No attacka esté woman," he said, as he turned me around and gave me a little nudge back into the bar.

I went back to sit beside Pete. It looked as if we were both going after some questionable women, just as my father had. There goes your self-control, I said to myself.

"Well, so much for that," I said. "It must be her sister, or someone."

"Maybe so," Pete said. "Now it's your turn to forget a beautiful woman, I guess . . . You know, I bet I could've found something out about Grandpa from Rosa. She's beautiful, smart, and a nice girl, too. That's all that I know. Maybe she's a little bit screwed up, but I can help her change."

"Maybe we'd better stay right here in the bar, where some other people are watching what happens? The vibes are bad in here."

The three men in dark suits had moved to stand against the wall, in front of the disc jockey, who was in a glassed-in booth lit by a red light bulb. One of the men stood in the red light with the other two. He had pockmarks all over his face, like a thousand little comets had hit him. She walked over and said something to the man with the scars and went back the booths in the darkness, while all three men watched all of the girls and all of their horny customers. It looked as if the three were the pimps, or maybe the owners of the place and the pimps, too. Six other men and one man and woman sat at the tables around the stage and watched the next dancer, who wore a gold sombrero and held two cap guns that she fired at the crowd. The whites of the watchers' eyes glowed in the black light.

Another girl came over and sat down next to me. It was a parade. They wouldn't give up, you had to give them that. She had dark hair and a great body along with what seemed to be an honest smile.

The cowgirl started strutting around on the stage and then swinging around the pole and stripping all the way down to her gold sombrero. The girl beside me reached over and started rubbing my thigh, and I took her gently by the wrist. Down boy, I thought. Take her easy. Self-control, please.

"Not tonight, my dear," I said. "Let's just talk." I waved a twenty in front of her face.

"You maricon?" she asked. "You queer man?"

"I'm just a nice guy who wants to talk," I said.

"A veces I like talk," she said, taking the bill from my hand and stuffing it between her breasts.

"See this viejo? Did you ever see him around here?" I said.

"No talk," she said. "First mas dinero. Por mi familia," she said.

"So how much more do you want?" I said.

"Tengo muchas hijos," she said. "Y mi abuella es muy pobre."

"Who doesn't have a giant family to feed in here?" I said. She looked about twenty. Another child hostage, I thought.

"It's a tough job you have working in a dump like this," I said.

"Hay worser jobs . . .You want come with me?" she said.

"Otra vez. Look at this photo. Did you see this man in the last two days or so?" I handed her the photo and ten dollars more. Some matches were on the table, so I lit one to give her a little light.

She turned the photo toward the match and looked at it.

"Jes, I see him," she said. "But he have one hat like from Vietnam--green, like Francais man." She stuffed the other ten between her breasts with the twenty. "He gives me mucho dinero, like last time he comes, and he says that he comes and takes us all to Disneylandia y Universal City y Hollywood. You maybe take me to Disneylandia y Universal City, like this old man say. Este viejo gustas these womens mucho. El dice que one day he take me to his hacienda for ride caballos. No just me, many girls. Muy rico este hombre. Es un coyote, or un rico gringo, or something? Tiene dinero como un bandito. Quien es?"

"My father," I said to her. "It sounds like it was Pop," I said to Pete. "You're sure that it was this man?" I asked her.

"Me no make lie," she said. "He comes from California, y everybody, he say, comes from los constellationes, he say. He likes jokes, I think." Then she pointed at the ceiling with her finger and made a circle in the air. "Poquito loco, pero amable," she said and laughed.

"When was this?" I said. "How many days?"

"Dos semanas," she said and looked over toward the men near the booth. "Too much talking," she said. "Pay mas dollares y Eduardo maybe no is angry."

A shadow approached from behind me. I looked back and

it was the pimp with the scarred face. He leaned over and whispered, "What . . . do . . . you . . . want . . . with . . . my . . . womens?" The words fell out of his mouth like ice cubes. He'd poured a bottle of two-dollar cologne on his head, and the smell made me gag.

I picked up my bottle of beer. "I just want to talk to this lady for a few more minutes more, finish this beer, then get the fuck out of here," I said.

Scar stared at me, then turned and walked back to stand against the wall as he had before, the red light from the glass booth framing him and the other two men.

"This is Eduardo," she said. "He has angry."

"That's one very evil man," I said. "If he's your boss, you should get a new one. He even smells evil."

She smiled and laughed again. "You get me uno mas cognac now, por favor? OK? This makes Eduardo happy."

"The old man. Did he say where he was going?"

"Maybe el vas a las estrellas. Maybe es un space man. Maybe you esta one space man, tambien," she said and laughed, her white teeth shining in the black light. "Este rico viejo tienes eyes blue like ocean y muy bonito. He wants take me to Universal City y Disneylandia." She looked at me with a sincere expression. "Por favor. Maybe you take me with you? Maybe you come and get me, then you take me to Universal City y Disneylandia?"

She waved the waitress over and asked her for another cognac.

What in the hell was my father talking about? Yeah, he was from the stars, all right, and he was flying around Mexico without a spaceship.

The waitress brought the cold tea, and I sipped my warm beer, and Scar stared at us. I wondered what was going to happen when Pete and I got up to leave. Rosa had no doubt told Scar that I hadn't given her more money. This is stupid, I thought. It wasn't a good idea to take your son to a whorehouse and put temptation on his plate, no matter who or what you were looking for.

"A donde viene el viejo?" I said.

"Es posible Marzo," she said and laughed again, then walked away, the fresh drink in her hand.

"Maybe so," I said.

I stood up and waved the waitress over to pay, and she brought the check to me in a ragged, plastic folder.

"A hundred and thirty-five dollares?" I said. "That's a little high for two beers and three cognacs. How much were the drinks?"

"Quince dollares cada uno cerveza," she said. "Cognac es veinte dollares cada uno," she said.

"Cognac muy fino? My ass. For Christ's sake, don't you people have any scruples?" Why ask? I thought. Of course they didn't.

"Y taxo turistica," she said. "Cover charge por el teatro, el baile moderno, y la Tahiti dancing."

"Modern dance and Tahitian dancing?" I said. "This place isn't Papeete, is it?"

"Si," she said. "Is normal price for girls y sexy dancing."

"I guess everyone gets screwed in this place, one way or another," I said.

If we refused to pay, I figured the suits would make sure that we didn't get out of there, so I gave her the money, along with a fifteen dollar tip, just to keep her happy and to keep the werewolves at bay. This was how they made up for what we didn't give Rosa and the other women. They probably would have charged us too much even if I'd given Rosa the other hundred bucks. That was their job.

Scar and the other two men in suits had moved to stand near the door. Pete and Rosita and I stood, and Rosita stepped back into the shadows and disappeared. The three suits and the bouncer watched us and waited, it seemed, for us to pass them on our way out. They looked as if they were ready to stop us. The bouncer at the door was the same guy from before. In the red light, I saw that his head had a tattoo of a skull with a black rose in its teeth. He smiled at us, and his cigar sent a gray ribbon into the air ahead of us as we walked toward him. The old Colt .45 would be nice to have in my pocket right now, I thought.

"Here's the whole damn congregation," I said.

Scar grabbed me by the arm. "You one cheap gringo. You no pay Rosa one hundred dollares mas."   ·

"She got all that my son had, one hundred dollars," I said.

"Is three hundred for cheap pendejos, como ustedes," he said.

The bald bouncer stepped toward me and looked at me, ready to smash me like I was a pumpkin.

"Next time you pay more," Scar said, still holding my arm. "Three hundred dollares. You one lucky hombre today. Lucky I am one very nice hombre."

"There won't be a next time," I said.

I grabbed his wrist and removed his hand from my arm. He bristled like a rabid dog.

His garlic breath and cheap cologne made me gag all over again. "Pinche gringo bastardos," he said.

"Adios, caballeros," I said.

We made it to the street, Scar and the big bouncer right behind us on the sidewalk.

"I guess you're right. They're a bunch of bandits," Pete said. "Poor little Rosa. All of those women are probably really nice, if you get to know them."

"They're the worst kind of bandits. For some reason I doubt that they're all 'really nice.' They're like white slavers. That damn place is a slave ship. I should've known better."

"It sounds as if Grandpa got around when he was here. He must've given them a pile of money."

"Hell, we gave them a pile of money, too. Pop must've really poured it on," I said. "I think we're lucky we got out of there alive. And so was he. That last girl might have really seen him. At least she knew that he has blue eyes. That's something.

Anyway, Pop's nuts, so he will do damn near anything and go damn near anywhere."

The three men in suits and the bouncer watched us from the doorway.

"Buenos . . . noches," Scar said, giving us the finger. "Cheap fucking gringos."

I took a deep breath, glad to be out of there. I could smell the ocean even over the cheap perfume that the girls had left all over me and the pimp's crappy cologne, which seemed to follow me down the street like The Blob.

"What did that girl say about him?" Pete said.

"She said that Pop told her that he was from the stars," I said. "But they thought that he was a Coyote, or someone from a drug family, because he had a lot of money to spend. Maybe we can believe her. He might have told her he was Joaquin the bandit, and she filled the rest in. He'll say anything he can think of when he's flying."

"Rosa is wonderful," Pete said. "I think I could've stayed with her for a long time."

"One maniac in the family is enough," I said. "Just be glad you got off with only a hundred bucks."

From Pichilingue we took the ferry across the Sea of Cortez to Mazatlan, where we spent a night, then drove south as long, as far, and as fast as we could without falling asleep at the wheel. We were heading for Jojutlan, on Lake Chapala, where my father had been born. In the jungle in Nayarit, we drove through a thunderstorm, and the road was covered with frogs, so we slid along on the highway at seventy miles an hour as if we were driving on Vaseline for a couple of miles. After that, the smell of frogs wafted up from the undercarriage of the van, so I pulled into a stream and drove backward and forward in the water to try and wash the frog guts off the belly of the van. But even after that, the smell stayed with us all along on the road south.

18

Dust billowed up from the cobblestone street and a dozen chickens scattered as we drove into Jojutlan, the place my father's family was from. A man wearing a black sombrero and a black charo suit galloped toward down the middle of the street on a black stallion. I steered around the vaquero and the chickens and rolled into the center of town and the zocalo. An old, black hearse with black fringe around the windows passed us and slowly drove out of town. The man on the black horse followed it. The horse's hooves clicked on the cobblestones. Then an old Thunderbird, brown and dirty, just like Cindy Paquette's car, came whizzing down the street, past us and the hearse, and out of town, leaving a cloud of smoke hanging above the street behind it.

"Jesus," I said. "That looks like Cindy's T-Bird."

"Cindy who?" Pete said.

"A woman that I know up north," I said.

"Not likely. It's probably someone else's car."

"You're right. She couldn't be down here."

There was a sign above a shop that said Farmacia Catalpa. My father had sent a card from here, too. My grandfather and a few hundred years of Catalpas had come from this town. The big hacienda and the horses had been here, in the old days.

I parked, and we both got out and walked into the pharmacy. Behind the counter, a young woman dressed in a white smock stood a few steps up a ladder. She was putting some boxes on a high shelf, and she turned and looked at us and smiled.

"Pardoname," she said and climbed down the ladder and stood behind the counter. She then smiled and said, "Can I help you, señor?"

"Por favor," I said. "My name is Sabas Catalpa. We have come to see Efrain Catalpa, my cousin."

When she heard my name, she looked me as if she was looking at a dead man, and her face turned white.

Then she regained her composure. "Seguro, Señor," she said. "Don Efrain is out at the farm. But his house is across the street, and you can wait for him there. The maid is there, I think." She came out from behind the counter and called to someone in the back that she was leaving for a few minutes.

"Come with me, please," she said, and we all went out the door and down the street.

When we got to a boarded up movie theater, the boards worn and the nails rusty, we stepped off of the boardwalk and went through a doorway and up some stairs to a balcony circling a garden full of ferns, flowers, and trees, which made a cool island of shade. Around the balcony were six green doors, and toward the back, we went into a living room with a black leather couch and a couple of easy chairs.

The young woman said, "Please sit. I'll get the maid for you." She went into another room that looked as if it was the kitchen and came back with an Indian woman who wore a white apron with a long skirt under it and had a long braid down her back. She looked as if she was thirty-five or forty. The woman from the pharmacy thanked us and went down the stairs, and the Indian woman said, "Do you want something to drink, señores?"

"Por favor," I said, and she went back through the door and then brought us some water which had small, lavender flowers in it, giving it a sweet, lemony taste. A mockingbird hopped around in a cage next to us as we sipped the cool drink. Then the woman brought us jicama with lime on it, and we waited. I knew Efrain from ten years before, when he'd visited us in California, but I didn't know how much he'd changed. I hoped he'd recognize me.

After an hour, steps came up the stairs, and it was Efrain. He'd gained twenty or thirty pounds, probably from drinking too much beer and tequila, and his face was more round, but he looked almost the same as I remembered him. He smiled at us and said, "Hola, primo!" He hugged me, then Pete. He had blue eyes, like my father's, just as I remembered.

"So my gringo cousins are here," he said and laughed.

"So how are you?" I said "Good to see you. You know Pete. He was little when you saw him last."

"He's not little now," he said. "He's a man. It's good to see both of you." He patted me on the back, then told the woman, "Bring us some tequila, Veronica, por favor." We all sat down in the dining room, and she brought out a bottle of Herradura and three glasses.

"Why didn't you tell me when you were coming?" he said as he filled our glasses with tequila. "Now I will call my brother and sister to come from Guadalajara so that they can see you. You must stay for a few days."

"Maybe," I said. "We didn't know that we'd get this far south so soon. But we do have to catch up to my father."

"Don't worry so much. You can catch up to your father any time," he said. "He was here last week for a few days. We had a good time talking about the past, and the old hacienda, and drinking a lot of tequila and Tecate," he said and laughed. "Your father said that someone from the family might come here looking for him. But he wasn't sure who it would be. He is very happy now, I think, more happy than I've ever seen him."

"I think that he's a little bit too happy," I said.

"Maybe so. Who knows?" he said. "But I will call the family again. They were happy to see your father, and they'll be happy to see you."

"Sorry that we didn't let you know we were coming. We weren't sure where we might catch up with him. He's been sending us weird postcards and letters for a couple of months, from all over the place. So we didn't know where we might find him."

"Okay," Efrain said, "I know that maybe he is a little bit crazy. He said something about taking back the all of the land that was taken from Mexico when we had the war with the gringos. I just laughed and told him that he was loco, that he would need a very big army. He said that if Mexico ever took it back, just think what we would have--Disneyland, and Hollywood, and Universal City, and the Grand Canyon, and Monument Valley. And all the blonde surfer girls in California. We would even get the Alamo, in Texas. And San Francisco, and the Golden State Bridge, and all of the baseball players, and the basketball players. And even the Victoria's Secret girls. Anyway, now he's going someplace down south, looking for some land, he said. I told him that it was very dangerous down there, that there are some crazy revolutionaries in the mountains. But he didn't seem to care. He said he had a lot of appointments to keep. I didn't ask him who he was going to see. But I told him to be careful."

"Appointments?" I said. "Disneyland? He told some whores in La Paz that he'd take them all to Disneyland and Universal Studios."

"Yes, I know that he says some funny things," he said. "He just wants some land and some horses, like his father and his grandfather had, like all of the family before had, in the old days. I think that he'll come back and maybe buy some land from us right here near Jojutlan. Maybe he can bring some of the Victoria's Secret girls to Jojutlan," he said and laughed. "I think that is a good idea, too."

"Did he say if he's coming back here?" I said.

"Yes, he's coming back. He wants to get some horses--Arabians, and Andalusians, I think. I told him that now we have more Ford Mustangs and Broncos than horses." He smiled at his own joke and took a sip of his tequila. "Your father wants to go

141

back to the old days."

"It seems as if he's already in the old days," I said. "He thinks he's Joaquin Murrieta and Paul Gauguin, and probably a few other guys. He thinks he can read the cave paintings in Baja. He's running like a mountain lion, out of control."

"He's old," Efrain said, "so he can be anyone he wants. He probably went through Michoacan, then south. That was ten days ago. But before he left I took him to our old ranch, and he loved it there. He felt like he was home. Maybe you'll like it there, too."

"We can't stay for very long," I said. "We have to catch up to him before he ends up in jail."

"All right, but stay two or three days," he said. "Who knows, he might come back tomorrow? He knows that it's muy tranquilo here in Jojutlan."

"I'm tired and I'm drunk enough for tonight," I said. "So excuse me. I need some sleep. We'll talk when we're sober."

"Good," Efrain said. "You two will love to eat and drink at the old hacienda with some of the family. I will arrange for them to come."

"Maybe," I said. "We need a couple of days rest, for sure."

Efrain showed us to two extra bedrooms that each had a green door that opened out on the balcony. In the room where I was to sleep, the bed was made, no doubt by the Indian woman, and I closed the door and lay down. We had driven four hundred miles that day. I closed my eyes, and I saw all of my Mexican ancestors there above me in the room, swirling in a blue mist, the Spaniards, the Toltecs, and a few other dead Indians.

The next morning, I saw that the left rear tire of the van was worn and some steel bands showed, so we needed a new tire. Efrain took me to a shop where we could get one, then said he was going to see how his horses were. The man in the tire shop said he had to get the tire from Guadalajara. It looked as if we had to stay there for a couple of days, that or put the spare on

142

and chance going to Guadalajara ourselves, so we decided we would wait.

When we got back to Efrain's place, he was sitting at a table in the kitchen.

"I called my brother, and my sister, and my mother, and some other cousins," he said. "They're all coming to the hacienda to see you, tomorrow at two. You have to stay for a little more time."

"Sure," I said. We had to wait for the tire, so we weren't going anywhere. "We'll be here a of couple of days. The llantero said that it will take two, maybe three days for him to get a tire."

"Good. It's fate. You are going to stay a few days longer," Efrain said. "Now you'll meet some of your family, and you can see my horses and ride them a little bit."

, , ,

At four that afternoon, we went into the family's muebleria with Efrain. They sold farm implements and tools, hay and wire, the normal stuff for a hardware store, and it was the place where the people who worked on Efrain's land came to get paid. He said he had to pay some of the field workers that day, a Friday. Inside, there were six men and six boys, who he said worked in the family's fields. An old man with a white mustache worked behind the counter there, and Efrain introduced us, and we shook the old man's hand. Pete and I sat there on a couple of barrels and watched Efrain figure out how much money the men and the boys who waited there were all going to get for the week's work.

Efrain got a notebook and a pencil from behind the counter, licked his thumb, and thumbed through the pages.

"Everybody has worked very hard all week," he said. "So it's one hundred pesos a day for the men and eighty pesos a day for the boys. That is five hundred pesos for the men and four hundred for the boys."

"We did as much work as the men," a boy in a red t-shirt said. "We should get as much as the men."

All of the other boys nodded their heads and talked to each other. The men just sat there without speaking, as if they were not concerned about their sons' pay. They acted as if they'd heard nothing that was happening.

"This is the way it always is," Efrain said. "The men get twenty pesos a day more than the boys. The men do more work than the boys."

The boys all shook their heads and started to jabber to each other about not getting paid enough for a day's work. I understood most of what they were saying.

"Yes," another boy said, "we should get a hundred pesos. We do just as much work as the men."

All of the boys jabbered at each other again, and Efrain smiled and said, "No, this is the way it is. One hundred for the men, and eighty for the boys." He smiled again.

A broom stood against the wall next to him, and he picked it up and tapped the boy with the red shirt lightly on the head. When he did that, he smiled and laughed.

Then the boy said, "It has always been this way, but it has been wrong. We always do as much work as our fathers." The boy smiled and laughed, too, as if he was just playing around. The boys all looked over at us sitting there on the table. They saw that they had a chance to force Efrain into paying more money, since we were his guests and were there to see what was happening, and Efrain would get embarrassed and give the boys more money.

"Yes," another boy said. "We want pay that's equal to the men's." The boy with the red shirt said, "Twenty pesos more!"

Efrain again touched the first boy on the head with the broom. Then the boy said, "You are cheating us. We are boys but we work hard."

Then Efrain lifted the broom and swung it hard through the air, and the boy dodged it and ran away from him down the

144

aisles of the store, Efrain running after him and swinging the broom, trying to hit him. Efrain's face was red, and his eyes looked angry as he chased the boy through the aisles, where there were big bolts of rope, shovels, boxes of nails, and bags of cement.

"You'll get what you always get, " he yelled. "Eighty pesos a day. It's what you always got and what you always will get until you are men."

Efrain swung the broom at the boy again and chased him out the door and into the street, and I could hear the boy yelling that he wanted more money as he ran away. Efrain came back into the store, and he was breathing hard and his face was red and covered with sweat as he looked over at us.

"That boy is always trouble," Efrain said. When he caught his breath he said, "He thinks that he does a man's work, but he's still a boy." He wiped the sweat off of his forehead with his hand.

"Sure," I said, "I see what you're saying. But it would be easier just to give the kids the extra pesos."

"Impossible!" he said. "We are the bosses, not the boys."

"Maybe they do just as much work as their fathers."

"We run the farm, not them, like always," he said.

Then Efrain pulled a roll of pesos-notes out of his pocket and began to pay each of the men, then each of the boys, who grumbled some more. But they weren't as brave as the boy in the red shirt, and they accepted the eighty pesos per day. Then they all walked toward the door, out into the shade of the late afternoon. It was probably still the same as when first the Toltec kings, then the Aztecs, and then the conquistadors, had run things, a few centuries back, the kings and captains on top, and the peons below.

The next day, we looked around at the old adobe buildings of the town, and, at two in the afternoon, we climbed into Efrain's old Ford pickup and drove out to the edge of town

145

where the old Catalpa hacienda had been. The only thing different in Jojutlan from a hundred years before was the cars parked in front of some of the houses and shops, where horses had once stood. Efrain wore a white cowboy hat, and he had a chromed .47 Magnum revolver in a holster on his hip. With the hat and the gun, he looked like a little fat guy who was trying to be a cowboy, a character out of a cartoon, but I didn't look at him much so I wouldn't laugh. I figured that he might shoot the pistol at some cans or something when we got to the hacienda.

"I can have a .47 Magnum like this because I am a member of a special government police," he said. "I can carry this pistola anywhere, but most people can't have pistolas. They can have only shotguns and rifles for hunting."

We drove past some ruins of a big building covered with vines that Efrain said had once been where they processed sugarcane.

"The Catalpa family has been ranching and farming sugarcane around Jojutlan for five hundred years," he said. "But after the revolution they sold the hacienda and a house in town to the Soto family, because all of the Catalpas were broke. The Sotos had been in Jojutlan almost as long as the Catalpas, and the two families have coexisted but also competed with each other. The Catalpas always wanted the land back, so we waited, and two years ago my sister Berta got married to a Soto, so the land and the hacienda and the old house in town are once again in the Catalpa family," Efrain said.

We drove between some tall trees on a dirt road. There were some muddy places, but Efrain skillfully went around them. The man with the black sombrero on the black horse went by us quickly.

"Who is that man on the black horse?" I asked Efrain.

"He's nobody, just old Vicente. He always rides around fast like that, the crazy old bastard," Efrain said.

Soon, you could see an old adobe house up on the hill, and Efrain pointed up and told us that this was the old hacienda.

Half of the adobe walls had crumbled, so only half of the big house still stood. There were old, red clay tiles on the roof and many arches. Efrain said that an Indian man and his wife and children lived there and took care of Efrain and Berta's husband's Arabians and Andalusians, which were kept in the adobe stalls there. Half of that building looked as if it was crumbling, too. It all looked as if it had been there for four or five hundred years.

A little further along the road, he parked and we got out. A young Indian man and his wife were there, but no one else. The woman was lighting some coals in a barbecue made from a fifty-gallon steel barrel. She had some meat in a bowl there, and she shooed the flies off of the meat as she said hello and smiled. The young man walked with Efrain toward where we could see the horses in their adobe stalls.

"Everyone isn't here yet, but they'll be here soon," Efrain said. "My wife is working in the pharmacy, but maybe she'll come for a little while, too. But meanwhile you can ride a couple of my horses."

The smell of horses and hay was strong near the adobe stalls. Efrain told the Indian man who worked for him there to saddle the two black Arabians. While the Indian man did so, Efrain showed us his gray and black Andalusians. All of the horses had just been brushed, and their black and gray coats shined in the sun. The Indian man saddled two horses, and when he was done, Efrain pointed out which horse each of us should get on, and we mounted.

"You two can ride, can't you?" Efrain said.

"Sure we can," I said.

"Ride out across that field to the ruins and look down from the hill on Jojutlan," he said.

We headed through the high grass across field. Efrain, the Indian man, and the man's wife stood and watched us as we rode out into the high green grass, which ran all the way down to the lake. We rode up to the top of a hill, where there was a view of

147

more farmlands and the adobe ruins of a building where they had processed the sugar. You could see some of Jojutlan to the south. Beyond the town and the farmland, Lake Chapala lay like a polished, blue stone that went on for a hundred miles or so and shone like glass in the sun. For a minute, as we sat there, I felt that I knew what my father was looking for in the past. I sat on the horse and looked down toward the lake that Efrain had told us was now very small, because they'd had very little rain. I pictured the conquistadors that had first come there, all wearing helmets and armor, all sweating in the heat. It looked as if Pete might have been seeing them in his head, too, since he looked like he was in a dream as he rode the black mare. This ride is about as close to inheriting horses as we'll ever get, I thought.

When we got back to the hacienda, there were tables set up in the shade of a tree, and Efrain's mother, Esmerelda, and his brother, Miguel, were there, along with my grandaunt, my grandfather's sister, Trinidad, and a young woman named Anna, who was a professor at the university in Guadalajara and a cousin, somehow. Miguel said he was glad that we had come, and he was glad he could come to Jojutlan for a few days to see us, and it was good for him to get away from Gualdalajara. Then Berta and her husband, Ramon Soto, drove up in their black Lincoln and parked and got out and sat down at the long table with us. We all sat there in the shade, eating the carne asada and beans and handmade tortillas that the Indian woman cooked, and drinking beer and a little tequila. Berta's husband, Ramon, played the guitar and sang a couple of songs, but he was a terrible singer, and it was hard not to laugh, but I managed to keep myself from laughing. He and Efrain looked like a comedy team.

"This is the way it was in old days," Efrain said. "When the Catalpas were first here, the first patron was called Sabas, like you, and he was a tax collector here and in Michoacan. When he came by ship from Spain, he had his wife and her sister and his two boys, a woman to care for the boys, two men who

148

worked for him, and three Indian slaves. His carriage was the first one that had ever been brought by ship from Spain to Vera Cruz."

I pictured a Spaniard with a goatee and a mustache, who smoked a big cigar while he rode around in his black carriage pulled by four black horses. On the seat beside him sat a box full of Indian gold idols and jewelry, and behind the carriage, a couple of Indians ran after it. My Spaniard ancestor, Efrain said, collected money from everyone, then took his percentage as pay and put it in his pocket.

"Did my great-grandfather leave anything for my father?"

"Probably so," Efrain said, "but I don't know what it was."

That sounded familiar.

He took a drink of his tequila and looked out across the cane fields and the farmland, beyond the old hacienda and the lake.

"All of this is our land." He pointed his finger to his left and moved it all of the way to his right. "And back there, too." He motioned behind him. "We lost some of it for a while, but now we have it all back, thanks to Ramon and Berta."

Ramon and Berta smiled and Ramon strummed a guitar.

"Did my father like your horses?"

"He liked all of them a lot," Efrain said. "He rode my black Arabian for a whole afternoon, and he loved it. Catalpas always have good taste," he said and laughed.

"That's probably as close as he'll ever get to owning an Arabian."

"Maybe so," Efrain said. "But anything is possible. With luck, he'll get some horses some time. Catalpas are very lucky about horses. Maybe it is the same in the north?"

Berta pointed at me and said, "Look at his nose. It's just like Aunt Trinidad's."

"I have my father's nose," I said. "That's what everyone says."

149

"Yes," Aunt Trinidad said, "you have a wonderful Catalpa nose, and your father has a wonderful Catalpa nose, too, just like my beautiful Catalpa nose."

"Do you remember my grandfather?" I asked her.

"Oh, yes. My father had a nose like mine, too," she said. "And your grandfather had the same nose. I remember when the revolutionaries were coming one day, Sabas and my father put all of the women in big canoes and sent them out to Alachran Island, in the middle of the lake, and when we got there, we had to stay in the boat with the water around us, because there were scorpions all over the island, just like its name suggested, and we didn't want to be stung. When the Villistas finally left, we came back to Jojutlan, but every time the guerillas and the Villistas came, they put the women in the canoes. My mother got angry at my father for hiding his black Arabian stallion in her bedroom, because she had the statue of the Virgin in there and she was afraid that the horse would break it. I have that statue still," she said, and smiled, then sipped her jamaica. "Your father has a Catalpa nose, and you have one. And your son has a Catalpa nose, too."

I looked over at Pete and then Efrain and scratched my Catalpa nose. I pictured a hacienda grande full of horses and big Catalpa noses all in a line, like a nose army.

"She can't hear very well," Efrain said. "Don't mind her. She is hearing questions that no one asks, and she is always in the past, somewhere, when she talks."

"I guess you always inherit something," I said

"Of course you do," Efrain said. "And your children inherit something else from you."

"I guess that a nose is useful," I said.

She agreed, and we all smiled and sat there talking for a few hours more, surrounded by the ruins, our noses all a matching set.

Efrain and his wife Lena stood next to the van the next morning, and we shook his hand and gave each of them a hug goodbye. They were nice people from a nice little town.

"Thank you for staying," Efrain said. "It was a very good time. You know, my father had something to give to your father, that his father had said he inherited, but I don't know what is was."

I keep hearing that line, I thought.

"Sure," I said, "a lot of time has passed since then. It's hard to know what it was, I guess. Oh well, I guess we all got Catalpa noses."

Efrain laughed. "Of course. You are always welcome," he said. "This is your house."

I figured he had told my father the same thing, since some horses and some land might have been his, if he had stayed here instead of going to the states with his mother. It would have been very different. Anyway, the whole thing had been settled without him, expediently, and that is the way it went.

"Wait, I forgot something," Efrain said. "I have to give you a journal that your father left here."

He went into the house and came back with a beat-up journal that had my father's name written on the inside cover. I thumbed through the pages. Some of his writing was in it, along with some sketches that looked as if they were of places that he'd seen on the road. It was like the postcards that he had sent, only there was more writing. I'd take a closer look at it down the road.

We thanked Efrain and Lena again and then waved at them as we drove out on the cobblestone street.

There at the edge of town sat the man with the black sombrero on his black horse. He tipped his hat to us as we passed. I waved at him, and he smiled and galloped back into town.

Further out, there was a field of high grass that went on for

151

a quarter mile, then an old cemetery with a wrought iron fence around it, and Pete said he wanted to look to see if any Catalpas were residents there. We were a mile or so out of town. There was a flock of white tombstones along with white marble crypts built to look like small Greek or Roman temples, others with crosses and sculptures of angels, and others just stone tablets. All lined up in rows, the tombstones looked like little buildings, as if the place was a miniature city for the dead. The cemetery was on four or five acres, and when I stopped the truck and got out to walk with Pete through the tombstones, we saw that the rain from the night before had made the dirt pathways muddy, and the wet clay stuck to the soles of our shoes as we walked along between the tombstones looking for Catalpas.

"That guy Vicente on the black horse is an antique," I said.

"He's a spooky old dude," Pete said.

We walked through the mud for half an hour, stopping to scrape the clay off of our shoes three or four times, before we finally found a white, marble crypt that said that it held Sabas Catalpa Garcia III, Sabas Catalpa Alvarado IV, and Sabas Catalpa Prieto V, along with their wives--Berta, and Elisa, and Camilla, and two more who were Efrain Catalpas, along with a few others. Wilted, red gladiolas were stuck in a vase attached to the wall of the crypt. Sabas Catalpa One had been born in 1640 and died in 1712. It looked as if he might have been the first Sabas of the family to be buried there. There were a few other Sabas Catalpas, then the grave of Sabas Catalpa Garcia VI, who looked as if he was my great-great-grandfather, and then Sabas Catalpa Estancia VII, who was born in 1893 and was my grandfather, the Federale paymaster who'd been caught by the guerillas and had his teeth kicked out for the gold. I remembered an old photo of him, lying twisted in the dirt, bruised and bloody, which someone had taken.

"This place is loaded with Catalpas," Pete said.

"They've been running this little town for a long time.

There were probably a few good guys, along with a few bast-
ards."

"Your dad's number eight. You're number nine, so I'm
number ten, I guess," Pete said.

"That sounds right. The rest of them must be in
another graveyard somewhere around here."

"I don't much like seeing my name on a tombstone."

"I don't either," I said. "They'll have to plant us somewhere, one of these days."

An old woman, wearing a black dress and a black rebozo
over her head and covering her face, came walking down the
path that we were on. When she passed us, she said, "Buenos
tardes, señores. You are here to see the Catalpas?"

"Yes, we are. How did you know?" I said.

"You are looking at the Catalpa grave, of course. And you
both have the Catalpa nose. Anyone can see that."

"We have a room full of Catalpa noses," I said. "You
must know the Catalpas well."

"Certainly I do," she said. "I worked for fifty years in their
house, until I was too old to work."

"I'm Sabas Catalpa," I said. "What is your name?"

"Bueno," she said, "señor Sabas. Elena Mendez Santana,"
she said. "There was a grandson that was taken by his mother to
California. Maybe that was your father?"

"That's right," I said.

"El patron always spoke of that grandson in California," she
said. "He wanted him to return to Jojutlan. He had things to give
him when he returned, twenty thousand gold pesos and many
horses, he said."

"That's the first I've ever heard about gold pesos," I said.
"He told you that?"

"No, he told me nothing," she said. "But I heard him
talking about it, many times. My memory is still good."

"What's your name again?" I said.

"Elena Mendez Santana," she said.

153

"How along ago did you stop working for the family?" I said.

"Ten years ago. But they still know me and they help me some to get by."

Her face was half-covered by her rebozo, only her eyes and her wrinkled forehead showing, as if she was wearing a mask.

"Do you know anything about the man on the black horse, Vicente? Why is he always riding his horse around town?"

"Vicente? He's your bastard uncle, the bastard of your grandfather," she said. "Now he just rides around town trying to scare people, the crazy old man. He is like a ghost. He has nothing but that horse and that black sombrero, and that charo outfit. Pardonome, señores, I have my family graves to tend."

She turned and walked down the path between the tombstones and toward the back of the graveyard and out of sight behind the old trees. I climbed up on top of the crypt and looked for her in the cemetery and the field beyond, but she wasn't there.

When we got back to the van, we scraped the clay off of our shoes with sticks, but we couldn't get all of it off, so our shoes were as gray as if they'd been painted. Then we drove along the western coast of the lake and into the green farmland of Michoacan.

We drove south, toward Oaxaca.

"What happened to all of these horses and this gold, do you think?"

"I think it all disappeared," I said. "And it won't be coming back."

I thought of the story my father had told me about, when he'd gone down to Jojutlan before I was born. His Uncle Efrain standing at the door. "Oh, Sabas. My father had something for you, but I don't know what it was."

Who gives a damn? I thought. The old lady was probably crazy. Gold pesos? It sounded like Don Ramon and his story about gold in the mountains. And horses? If you own a bunch of

154

horses, someone has to shovel the horseshit and babysit them when you're gone, I thought. It's just a lot of trouble. No, in truth they would be great to have, of course.

"Do you think that what she said is true?" Pete said.

"I think that it doesn't make any difference what she said. Those gold pesos are a long time gone," I said.

"Did Efrain say anything about it?"

"He might not even know anything about it," I said. "The family might not know anything about it. They were just kids when it happened, or not even born."

"What if Efrain did know?"

"Then he'd be a liar, I guess. But I don't think he knows any more than we do."

"He might, and he might not even want us to find Grandpa."

"I don't think he'd really care what we know about it. That all happened a long, long time ago."

"Did you look at that notebook yet?"

"I'll take a look at it later, when you're driving," I said. "We have a long way to go before we can sleep."

19

My father had told Efrain that he might go to a little town called Puerto Escondido, on the coast in Oaxaca, to look for some land to buy, so we drove south and then west. It was a long way south. I knew about Puerto Escondido. There were big waves there, a very big and very good swell, so the place had been in the magazines. We wound through steep mountains and snaking roads, and when we got to the top of the final pass and started down, there was jungle, thick and green and twisted. We drove days and spent nights in places along the road and in the van. Five days later, we got to Puerto Escondido just before sunset. We got a hotel near the beach. It had an old, spiral staircase and rooms with mahogany doors and window frames, and there was a view of the ocean at the end of the street. The place looked as if Pancho Villa might have stayed there when he and his army of Dorados, with their gold hats, had swung though.

From there, I didn't know which way we should go. All of the way down, we had asked a few people if they'd seen a man in a black cowboy hat, or any other kind of hat. No luck. I thought that we'd stay around there on the beach for a few days and ask around, see if we could find out if he'd been through there, and then go wherever that took us. In our room that night, I thumbed through my father's journal. As Pete had said, there were songs and their translations and some other things written there. One song was about Joaquin Murrieta. I'd heard it sung once by a mariachi in a cantina ten years before. I read through it all while looking at the translation that he'd written.

The Journal

El Corrido de Joaquín Murrieta

I am not American
but I understand Indians—
I learned about them from my brother
backwards and forwards,
and I can make any American
tremble at my feet.
When I was just a boy
I was left as an orphan
without anyone to care for
(later) my brother was killed
and my wife, Rosita,
how she was martyred
I have my gun in my belt
and my bandalero is full.

And I came from Hermosillo
in search of gold and riches.
The good and simple Indian
I defend with ferocity
The sheriff had put
a high price on my head.
I have been in every cantina
fighting Americanos.

You are the Captain
who killed my brother;
you caught him unarmed,
you proud American.
I was traveling in California
in the year of eighteen-fifty
with my pistol in my belt

157

and my bandalero full,
and I am the Mexicano
whose name is Joaquin Murrieta.
And we're going to make a raid.
It will be wild and fast
with plenty of horses
and I'm also bringing Three-
who has been a faithful friend.

After that, there was a letter to my mother that he hadn't yet torn out and sent.

Dear Margaret,

I'm in Loreto, where the sky is so clear that you can almost see all the way across the Sea of Cortez to Sonora. Or that's what it seems. I can see land across the water through the window of the cantina. But I know that it's Isla Carmen, not Sonora. They say that Joaquín Murrieta was from Sonora, and that his descendants are still there. I'd like to find them and find out where he really died, but I have other plans.

I'm going south to Jalisco and the old Catalpa hacienda in Jojutlan. My grandfather has left something for me, I am sure. He had six Arabian stallions and five Andalucians. Once, when some Villistas had come to town, he'd hid his favorite black Arabian stallion in his and my grandmother's bedroom. My grandmother hadn't wanted him to put the Arabian there with her statue of the Virgin, but he did anyway. The statue had been in the family for three hundred years. The Virgin made it through that night without being knocked off the table and broken by the stallion. And the Villistas hadn't thought to look in the bedroom for anything, so they hadn't seen the stallion. But when they left my grandfather brought the horse out of the bedroom, so my grandmother was relieved that her statue of the Virgin hadn't been broken.

For now, there are the pictographs on the cliff sides that I saw and am beginning to understand. I think that I know what they're saying. A professor from Guadalajara told me that those paintings of men and women with their arms held up in the air, as if they are being held up by someone, are really maps of constellations--Ursa Major, the Pleiades, Orion. They are made from the same stars that we make our constellations, or almost the same stars that we make ours out of, just with different configurations.

Some of our ancestors are leaving signs for us. First those paintings and then the song about Murrieta that the mariachis

159

were playing up in San Javier, that song that I hadn't heard in sixty years. They are telling me that the revolution of the Indian people is next. So first we'll take Mexico back, then concentrate on California and the rest of the Southwest. The road south to La Paz first goes west toward Magdalena Island and Magdalena Bay. There will be signs for me in La Paz. I'll take the ferry to Mazatlan, then head to Jojutlan to see the family and pay respects to the ancestors. Today I drove through the desert, past those tall cactuses curling like tentacles into the sky.

I have been watching for plainclothes agents who are following me. Who is this bartender, really? Who are those three men sitting at the bar? Are they agents of the gringos? They are here to watch what I'm doing. They're following me, to see if I find the men who will follow me as they did Murrieta.

This bar is made of old mahogany, dark, brown and red below the varnish, the wood carved. You can smell the tequila and beer that have been spilled on the floor on thousands of nights and yesterdays. The bartender has a Zapata mustache, high cheekbones. Mostly Indian blood runs through his veins. But it is probably a disguise. I know who he really is.

Behind the bar, two rows of bottles, and behind them a mirror with a long crack from top to bottom. Down in Jalisco, I can get an army of Toltecs who will head north with me. In Chiapas and Yucatan and Quintana Roo and Guatemala the Mayans are waiting for me. The Tarahumara wait for me in Chihuahua. They will be glad that Joaquin is back. I will tell them the truth, that he has returned, and they will come. We can take Mexico back from the Conquistadors and their children. Then get the north with the Aztecs, Toltecs, Zapotecs, Mayans, Tarahumaras, Huichole, Yaquis, and Apaches. All of the forty tribes of Mexico can come together to get rid of all of the conquistadors' children who are still running Mexico.

In the Colony, they told stories about Joaquin Murrieta, about how the miners had raped and killed his wife, then hanged his brother, and how Joaquin had then gone after all miners, to get

160

that it was their own fault that they had been cheated by the false agents. This could sometimes happen three or four times, and since the foreign miners had no recourse, they were forced to pay the tax over and over again. If a foreign miner refused to pay the tax to a valid representative of the government, he was ordered to leave his claim, so that his diggings could then be taken over by a white Forty-Niner.

During that same time, the Americans were in the process of killing off any Indian that they saw. A bounty of twenty dollars was offered for any Indian male's scalp. The scalp of a female or a child got a bounty of five dollars. Before Cabrillo's exploration, it is estimated that California had at least fifty separate tribes of indigenous people. First the explorers and then the Dominican fathers who established the California Missions brought with them diseases that the Indians' immune systems could not handle. By 1849, eighty percent of the Indians had died from diseases, brought first by the Spanish, and then by the white Americans, or they had had been enslaved by the Spanish, then finally killed for a bounty, during the Gold Rush, by the American miners who had come for the gold.

On May 11, 1853, California Governor John Bigler signed legislation authorizing a band of California Rangers, headed by Captain Harry Love, a former Texas Ranger, to go after Joaquin Murrieta and his band. After a year of near misses, they finally cornered what they were sure was Joaquin Murrieta and his friend, Three-Fingered Jack Garcia, and a dozen of his men, in the Tejon Pass, south of Bakersfield. After a day-long battle, Captain Love and his men finally shot and killed two men that they said were Joaquin Murrieta and Three-Fingered Jack Garcia. They promptly decapitated the dead man they considered to be Murrieta, then cut off the right hand of the other man, who had three fingers on his right hand, whom they pronounced to be Three-Fingered Jack Garcia. They put the head in a jar of cheap whisky, the hand in another jar. Then they took the jars to Sacramento and presented them to the governor as proof of their capture. He proudly displayed those trophies in his office for two years, until he was no longer governor. Captain Harry Love was first given $1,000 reward money, and later given a bonus of $5,000 more by the California legislature.

It is doubtful that Joaquin Murrieta and Three-Fingered Jack Garcia were the bandits that Captain Love and his rangers encountered and killed on that day in July of 1853. At the time, there were at least five Joaquins who were raiding and robbing Californian towns and mining camps; Joaquin Botellier, Joaquin Carrillo, Joaquin Ocomorenia, and Joaquin Valenzuela were a few of these. The head and the hand that the rangers had taken have surfaced in carnivals and in private collections, occasionally, over the last century, but it is believed now that they have since been destroyed by fire, misplaced, stolen, or simply lost.

There is a photograph that is either an ambrotype or a tintype of a man said to be Joaquin Murrieta. The ambrotype and the tintype were invented in 1854 and 1856 respectively, a year and two years after Joaquin Murrieta's reported death at the hands of Captain Love and his rangers. So if it is actually an image of Murrieta, then Captain Love received a reward for capturing and killing the wrong two men. The image is presently on display in an Old Timer's Museum in Murphy's, in Calaveras County.

Some say that it was not the correct Joaquin that Captain Love and his rangers killed that day in the Tejon Pass, but another Joaquin along with another man who had all of his fingers, who was positively not Three-Fingered Jack Garcia. Presently, the surname Murrieta is common to many people in a small village seventy-five miles outside of Hermosillo, in Sonora, Mexico. The many Murrietas who still live in that part of the Sonoran desert claim that they are the descendants of the famous bandit, Joaquin, but they have only their family stories as proof, so their veracity is inconclusive. Joaquin may have lived on for many years in the mountains and hills of California, or in Sonora, Mexico, where he is still loved and remembered and still a legend.

20

The Journal

one Luger
one Mauser
one .22 hex barrel pump
one .32 hex barrel pump
one .45 automatic
one Winchester .30-.30
one compound bow
25 hunting arrows
one Samurai sword

Ammunition
.22 long rifles
.32 longs
.30-.30's
Other Stuff
red serape
Black Stetson
pork tamales
beef tamales
Herradura tequila

Carabina .30-.30 .30

Carbine .30-.30

Carabina .30-.30
Que los rebeldes portaban
Y Decían los maderistas say
Que con ella no mataban not kill

Carbine .30.30
that the rebels carried
and the Maderistas
that with her they did

Carabina .30-.30
que rebeldes portaban
Me voy a marchar
y decían los maderistas say
que con ella no mataban not kill.

Carbine .30-.30
that the rebels carried.
I'm going to march
and the Maderistas
that with her they did

Con mi .30-.30 .30
me voy a marchar
a engrosar las fillas
de la rebelión
Si mi sangre piden, me sangre les doy
por los habitantes de nuestro nación

With my .30-
I'm going to march
to thicken the rows
of the rebellion.
If for my blood they ask
my blood I will give
for the inhabitants of
of our nation.

Questions:
    Who were the Painters?
    Where did they go?
    How did they paint the paintings so high on the
cliffs?
    Constellations of men and women:
    The women--breasts protruding from
    their arm pits, arms up in the air.
    The men wearing helmets, their arms in the air.
    Who are they waving hello to?
    Who are they saying goodbye to?
    Constellations formed in the shape of animals:
        The gray whale
        The manta ray
    ciervo
        borego
        mountain lions

Constellations and Star Clusters
Possible pictograph representations of:
The Pleiades
Ursa Major
Ursa Minor
Orion
Scorpio
Cancer
Cassiopeia

There was a section of the journal where it looked as if
some pages had been torn out by someone. You could see the
glue and the spine were exposed. I figured that my father must
have torn the pages out, but it could have been someone else. No,
I thought, Efrain wouldn't have done that.

167

Mother

My mother hasn't been back to Mexico since she left Jalisco, just before the revolution ended in 1918.

I asked her if she wanted to go back.

I said, "Come on, Mom. I'll take you down to Jalisco, and you can see your family and the old village and Guadalajara."

"No, I don't want to go down there," she said.

Back when she left Mexico, she took the train north to Mexicali and then came by bus from there to Orange County and The Colony. She was running away from both my rich grandfather and the revolution. My father, then a paymaster in the Federal Army, had just been killed by the Villistas. He had been carrying the payroll from place to place. After they killed him and his two guards, they kicked their gold teeth out and left him at the side of the road to rot. There's a photo of him lying on the ground, his broken face half bruised and twisted. I remember Mom showing it to me, but I don't know where that photo is.

"Come on, Mom, you'd love to see it now," I said. "You haven't been back there for fifty-five years."

"No," she said, "I don't want to go down there again. I don't want to see all of those dead men hanging from the telegraph poles," she said.

For a week now it has been hard for me to get up in the morning, and it is even more difficult for me to drive. I am fishing for something in dry sand, as someone said. I am looking down into the abyss, a hole in which there is no bottom, like the mirrored image when you sit in a barber's chair. I don't know when or if I will be able to climb the many miles out of it.

I wonder, Who is the Cisco Kid?

I lie awake all night wishing for sleep until the dawn comes and I pry myself out of bed and put on my clothes that are as heavy as lead. Then the next night comes and I lie here again, with my eyes forced closed until I go to sleep only for a moment until a lightning bolt runs through me and I am awake again

All along I wonder, Who is Pancho?

21

There was a palm-shaded stand where they sold cold drinks on the beach in Puerto Escondido, and we sat under a palapa and ordered two beers. We needed to sit and take it easy for a while. We'd asked around in the village about my father, but no one had seen anyone that looked like him around. It was hot and humid and my shirt was all wet with sweat, but we were in the shade and the beer was cold. The surf rolled in and over the reef of Puerto Escondido. Behind us, a dirt road wound up the hill, past a couple of houses with few palm leaf roofs and then into the jungle. A tall man wearing cut-off Levis and a white peon's shirt walked out of the jungle and straight to the shade of a palapa and a chair at the end of the row of chairs. He had a limp, and he wore guaraches, and he had a short beard. In his right hand, he carried a clear plastic bag with a drawstring that had a bottle of tequila and a pack of Marlboros in it. He looked like an American, and he looked as if he had been in Mexico for a long time. The woman from the cafe went over to him and asked what he wanted, and then she went to her cooler and brought him a beer, then went back and gave us each another beer, too.

"Son con los complimentos de el señor," she said and nodded toward the tall man.

"Thanks," I said and raised the beer bottle to him.

"Mind if I come down and join you?" he said. "I feel like talking to some gringos for a change."

"Have a seat," I said.

He stood and walked with a slight limp over to sit down below the palapa next to us. He put his beer down on the small table between us.

"Sabas," I said and shook his hand, "and this is my son, Pete."

"Tom Batey," he said, "not Tom Petty." He smiled and laughed. "Pleased to meet you."

"Looks like you live around here," I said.

"Yeah, up in the mountains," he said. "I have a little house and a farm up there."

"A farm? What kind of farm is that?" I said.

"Just a farm," he said, "like Old MacDonald."

"Oh, just a farm," I said. "How long have you been doing that?"

"Long enough," he said. "You here for the waves?"

"No, we're here to find my old man," I said. "He's down here somewhere south of T. J."

"There's a lot of Mexico south of T. J., amigo," he said. "But we have primo waves down here. Very big and very excellent."

"We saw the break way out there," I said. "It looks pretty big. We probably need to do a few more push-ups."

"You have your boards?" he said.

"Yeah, but we don't have the time," I said. "Anyway, it's really big out there. I probably need to do a few more push-ups to take that on."

"You ought to take a few hours and get wet," he said.

"Maybe, if it settles down a little. But we have other things to do."

We finished the beer and ordered three more. The air was hot and wet, and there was nowhere else that we could think of to go and cool off, except for into the water, where the waves looked to be fifteen feet or so. Way too big for an easy-going surf.

"You two aren't working for the feds, are you?" he said. "Or the DEA?"

"No, we aren't feds," I said. "And we're not DEA, either. Besides that, we're in Mexico, remember?"

171

"You can't tell about anyone anymore," he said. "I need a smoke."

"Have at it," I said.

He took the pack of cigarettes out of his plastic bag, took out a fat joint that was in the pack, and lit it up. He didn't seem to care what the woman who was serving us thought. And she didn't seem to care or even notice what he was smoking.

"Want a taste?" he said.

"Too early for me," I said.

"It's my recent crop. Primo stuff," he said.

"That's from the farm?" I said.

"Yep, Old Tom Batey had a farm, up-in-the-jungle-with-the-jaguars," he sang. "E yiii, E yiii, yoooo."

"You're being kind of flamboyant, smoking pot right here, aren't you?"

"Everybody around here knows me," he said. "They know what I do, too. They just like that I contribute to their economy and bring a lot of pothead turistas here, too. I'm good for tourism, man."

The woman behind the counter looked past us at a green sea without ships.

"Aren't there any cops here?" I said.

"Yeah, two of them," he said, "but my beautiful and estranged wife is the daughter of the head of the Federales for the whole damn country. And those two gendarmes know it."

"That's convenient," I said.

"I haven't seen her in two years," he said, "but she still loves little old Tom Batey. My charming personality's hard to resist. She is still in my entourage." He laughed like a tall, skinny Santa Claus.

"Does she know what you do for a living?" I said.

"Sure," he said. "I've been at it for years, ever since I left the war."

"Which war?" I said.

"The one before the last one," he said. "What if I take care

172

of some business, then meet you at the restaurant up the street with the big palapa? Three o'clock? The fish is pretty good."

"Sure, that sounds good," I said. "We'll see you then."

The restaurant under the big palapa was a place where a lot of tourists ate, a little fancy and trying to be fancier, as if the people who ran the place were waiting for Elizabeth Taylor and Richard Burton to walk in. They had real cloth napkins, hand-blown wine glasses, and red tablecloths.

"The huachenango's great here," Batey said.

So we all ordered the red snapper. The woman who served us looked at Tom as if he had something contagious, but she took his order, then left.

When the red snapper came, the whole fish, head to tail, was laid out on our plates. It was a good dinner, and we drank a couple of beers while we ate.

"Want to see a magic trick that gets me a free dinner?" Batey said.

"No, but I think you're going to show me," I said.

"Watch the magician work," he said. "THIS FISH IS DISGUSTING!" he yelled. "IT STINKS AND IT'S FULL OF FUCKING MAGGOTS!"

The woman who had brought us our food rushed over to our table.

She said, "Is there a problem, señor."

"Terrible!" he said. "It's just disgusting."

"What is the problem, señor?"

"This fish, it's making me sick," he said. "I think I'm going to barf. Man, I'm really sick."

"We're very sorry, señor," the woman said. "We will not charge you for your dinner, señor."

"You bet you won't," he said. There was one small bite of fish still on his plate.

"We will give you another dinner, señor. Please sit down,
173

señor."

"You couldn't pay me to eat here again today," he said and got up and walked out toward the beach.

We looked around at the people, who were now watching us as if we were the entertainment. I put two hundred pesos on the table, and we both got up and went out onto the muddy street.

When we caught up with Batey, he was laughing.

"Jesus Christ," I said. "That was cute."

"It works every time," he said.

"We sure as hell can't eat there again," I said.

"Sure you can," he said. "Don't worry about it. They know me in there. I've done that three times now. What can they say in front of the turistas? Besides, you paid for your food."

"They must really like to see you come in," I said.

He smiled. "They never do anything. They just want the turistas to be happy," he said. "I'll do it again, in a couple of months, and they won't say a word, just like today."

"That's a fun game," I said.

"It's entertainment, dude," he said. "We don't have much to do around here . . . Hey, why don't you guys come up to my place. I'll show you around. It's just a couple of miles up the road," Batey said. "What the hell."

"Can we trust you?" I said.

"Of course," he said.

"Let's go look around back there," Pete said. "It won't take long. We need a little break."

"If we go now, you can get back before dark," Batey said.

"All right," I said, "just for a couple of hours."

It was four o'clock, so we had a lot of light left in the day.

The dirt road through the jungle was covered by a canopy of limbs, their leaves hanging overhead, the shadows of the leaves on the dirt road as we walked. It was about two miles back, like Batey had said, a little house on stilts with a palm roof. I wasn't even sure why I'd said we'd come there, but we were

174

there.

"This is home," Batey said. "Come on in."

Inside, there was a roughhewn wood couch and some leather-covered chairs around a round table. There were a couple of bedrooms, and down the hill, there were some other thatched-roof shacks.

"Pulque?" he said. "It's fresh."

"Sure," I said. "I'll have some. I'm thirsty."

He got us both glasses and poured us some pulque from a ceramic jug. The white liquid looked like soapy water.

"Did you ever try this stuff before?" he said.

"Once, ten years ago," I said. "It's kind of like dish-water, as I remember."

"This is some of the best you can get," he said. "They were drinking this stuff when Cortez and those assholes arrived. They made tequila from this."

Outside the windows, I watched the rain come down hard. The birds were cawing and chirping. Then the birds stopped, and the rain pounded down on the tin roof.

"You should pick up some of my weed," he said. "If you did, you could sell it for a bundle up north."

"No, thanks," I said. "We don't need any more trouble."

"Too bad. What's your father doing down here?"

"He's on vacation, I guess you could say." I drank some of the pulque. It had an earthy taste and there were bits of some agave and some other plants in it, but I swallowed it all.

"How about some peyote?" he said. "You could chew some yourselves later on, or you might just take it up north and pay for your trip."

"No thanks, again," I said.

"Aren't you going to get wet before you leave?" he said.

"I thought we might give it a try," I said. "The swell down the beach doesn't look as huge as it does on this end. It's just six-foot faces. We can handle that. But twenty feet is just too damn big."

"Maybe it would be good exercise," he said.

I just looked at him and said nothing.

I finished the pulque, and he poured some more out of the jug into my glass.

"Just a little more," I said. Toltec beer, I thought.

"I'll go in and see you in the morning, before you go out," he said. "Have some coffee with you, maybe."

He told us how he had lived down there since he'd come home after being wounded in the war. He was in the army, Special Forces, he said, and he'd gotten pissed off at the government, so he'd moved down and started growing weed, taking the best seeds and growing plants from them, then the best from that crop, and so on.

"Hybrids," he said.

The room began to feel closed in, for some reason, and through the window, it was as if I could watch the trees and vines as they grew while the rain pounded the leaves.

"What in the hell was in that pulque?" I said. "I'm hallucinating."

Batey smiled and laughed, and it echoed off the walls there in the shack.

"You'll be okay," he said. "It's just some mushroom juice, man. Psylocybin. Just go with it, man. It's a light trip."

The rain stopped, and the birds chirped and squawked and cooed, the trees in the jungle hissing as the wind blew the thunder storm inland. The sounds echoed through the jungle.

"Jesus, Tom, we didn't want to eat any fucking mush-rooms," I said. "What the fuck were you thinking?"

"I figured I'd give you a gift. Comprende? A little side trip to Castaneda Land, so that you'd cool out," he said. "You'll be back down to normal in a few hours. Anyway, it's a bitching walk back to town after a mushroom or two, if you want to walk back now. I have a flashlight you can use. But if you go now, just take it slow and be careful of banditos."

176

"Shit, you're a maniac," I said.

He laughed some more, "Ho, ho, ho," the Santa Claus of the Oaxacan jungle.

"Let's get the hell out of here," I said to Pete. "I want to sleep somewhere there aren't any surprises. I'm flying."

"I kind of like this," Pete said.

"Great," I said.

"Just spend the night," Batey said. "You're tripping and the jungle might get a little too weird for you in the dark, if you get paranoid. Picture this, man: The Huicholes are stoned every day. They sprinkle peyote on their food like salt and pepper."

"Good for the Huicholes," I said. "We're going back to town tonight, Batey."

"That's cool, man. Do what you want. It's a free country. Most of the time."

So we started the walk back. The mosquitoes buzzed around us like miniature helicopters. The birds cawed and squawked, then went silent when the rain came. On the wet dirt road it was like a blackout, no moon, no stars, only a low, thick fog that left our faces and clothes wet, even more wet than we had been at the Circo Velasquez, and the trees moved over the road toward us from the dark. Then the sky cleared, and the dark jungle trees had crisp, razor-cut outlines that blocked out the trillions of stars, the starlight casting our shadows on the road as we walked.

"This is some great stuff," Pete said.

"I've got a tripper in the family. Be glad that he didn't give us acid," I said. "I guess if the Huicholes do it all the time we can do it for a few hours. 'Like salt and pepper.' Some salt and pepper."

"I wouldn't want to be like this all the time. That would be weird," he said.

"I guess that it helps them to make their art. Whatever the case , Tom's an asshole. You don't do that to someone you like."

"I like him, even if he is an asshole."

"You can't trust the s. o. b."

"I think that you can't trust anyone down here."

"That seems to be the case," I said.

The birds sang and whistled and cawed louder, and the sky above seemed as though we were looking through a huge colander of stars and clouds made of stars. By the time we got into town and went to the hotel, it was two-thirty in the morning, and we were tired, and we lay down on our beds to sleep. Then there were little Toltecs again, only this time they were in my head and I knew it, even though I could see them as they made a pyramid on my chest, then tumbled down, then piled up, and tumbled down again, over and over. I knew why they were there. One time my father had said, "We're part Toltec, from my mother's family. She's half Toltec, even though she doesn't want to admit it. She had a Toltec nose, before she had it whittled down and made into a Lucille Ball nose. She has dark skin under all of that white powder. That's where I got these cheekbones." He had smiled and laughed then, at his mother making Lucille Ball an idol, I suppose.

"We brought the boards, so we may as well use them," I said.

When we got up the next morning, we felt great, for some reason. So we drove the van down the beach a half mile or so, and then got out and unloaded our boards and put our trunks on. The waves were smaller, manageable, I thought.

"It looks like it's five or six foot faces," Pete said.

"I'm going to watch it for a while before I go in," I said. "I don't want any twenty foot surprises."

Pete just ran toward the water and waded in, then jumped on his board and paddled out beyond the break. I sat and watched the waves for five minutes, and the waves just came in at six or seven foot. Manageable.

The water was as warm as the air, and when I wadded in, it felt like I was getting into a bathtub. I paddled out to a place fifty feet south of Pete.

A set of four to five foot faces came in, and Pete and I took the second wave left. He carved the face of the wave as I went in a straight line left on my old Gordie. There was no fancy stuff with that big log. We both made it out and paddled out again over the next set.

It was easy going, and I was relaxed and feeling good about the world as I waited for the next set to take in. Then I looked out and saw a huge wave coming toward us like a huge fist, maybe fifteen feet, so I paddled like hell toward it, to then climb the face and go over it, then another face and over, and a third swell roared through. All along, Pete was beside me. I paddled as hard as I could to get over that set and back to something less intimidating. But on a fourth wave we both paddled as hard as we could, and when we didn't get over the top in time, the wave broke and pushed us down to the bottom, where we both grasped at the bubbling white water for what seemed like five minutes but was probably more like thirty seconds. There was no telling which way was up. I held onto my board and it finally surfaced like a submarine on top of the white water. The wave then dumped us both off in the shallow water, where we could wade toward the shore and to the beach. I lay down for a minute to make sure that I was on dry land and safe, with Pete beside me probably thinking the same thing. This I knew: we were glad to have survived and to be able to go back into the jungle and look for Pop, wherever he was, out there in his own white water. Then we just sat on the beach and watched the big waves roll in, break and shake the sand, and then roll in again.

We sat outside on the street, at the cafe next to the hotel, and we both ordered coffee and pan dulce. The van was all packed and ready to go, and we'd gotten wet, plenty, just as Batey had suggested. I took a sip of my coffee and looked out across the bay, toward a finger of land to the north. Then I heard the rumble of a car with an engine that was missing badly,

179

thumping and stopping and thumping and stopping. I've heard that sound before, I thought. I ran down the street and looked over to see an old, brown Thunderbird that looked just like Cindy Paquette's car. This car was unwashed, just as hers had been, and it was covered in a pale brown coat of Mexican dust, the windows so dirty that you couldn't see who was inside or who was driving. A black cloud of smoke billowed up behind it as it loped down the cobblestone street. I tried to see the license plate, to see if it was from California, but the car rumbled down the street, then around an old, white bus full of locals who looked as if they were going to work somewhere. No, I thought, you're hallucinating again if you think she's driving around way down here.

I ran down the street after the car. Then it turned left around the corner, so I ran to that corner. But there was just the green jungle up the hill, no car, just a big, fluffy cloud of Mexican dust. She's after me for sure, I thought. She has Grandpa's .45 that she stole from me, and she's going to shoot me. I was convinced that she was there, somewhere, waiting. Then I thought, Maybe it's still those damn mushrooms? You're paranoid. You're seeing things, I thought.

When I walked back, I found Pete still sitting at the sidewalk cafe, talking with our dear friend Tom Batey. Pete and Tom were smiling at me, for some reason, and drinking coffee. Tom's plastic bag with the drawstring and his tequila and other essentials was on the ground next to him.

"Hey, amigo," he said. "What's going on?"

"When did you show up?" I said.

"I rode my bicycle into town this morning, to check if you two made it," he said. "Some asshole put mushrooms in your pulque last night." He smiled a toothy smile, like Burt Lancaster. "You guys should've stayed at my place with me. It's dangerous out there at night. Jaguars. Banditos."

"That was a dirty fucking trick," I said.

"Yes, it was," Batey said. "I'm like that, a real Trickster
180

incorporated. Señor Raven. I just wanted to give you two a little trip, so that you'd remember old Tom. No harm done," he said. "I didn't put much in there. I didn't want you to fly too high."

"Thanks for being so considerate," I said.

"What were you running after?" he said.

"I saw an old T-Bird that looked like the one that this wacko woman has up north," I said. "But I couldn't catch it."

"How would she get way down here?" Batey said.

"Don't ask me," I said. "No telling what she'd do. She shoots people when she gets mad at them."

"It's not that woman, man," he said. "Take it easy. Have some coffee. This pan dulce has pineapple on it, just like in Paradise."

"Yeah," I said. "I don't know what I'm thinking, She couldn't be way down here. It was probably the damn mushrooms, thanks to Mister Ho, Ho, Ho, here."

"Man, there are a ton of old T-Birds down here," Batey said. "Anyway, you're way the hell out of range for any weird California chick."

"Sure," I said. "You're probably right. But it sure looked like her."

"These Mexicans down here love old T-Birds," Batey said. "You're just being paranoid."

"Maybe so . . . You missed watching us surf," I said. "We got knocked around a little by some waves."

"That's good," Batey said. "It's good to get whacked once in a while, just so she doesn't whack you too bad. Maybe you'll pay attention from now on."

"I guess you can never tell," I said.

"Like some old Indian said, 'It's a good day to die,'" Batey said.

The Journal

"Los Dorados de Pancho Villa."

Go to Chihuahua where Villa battled the gringos in southern New Mexico. The Columbus raids.

Villa's men who wore those gold sombreros were called Dorados.

The Dorados de Pancho Villa
I am the soldier of Pancho Villa
Of those Gold Sombreros I'm the most faithful
Nothing is more important than
But yes this is the thing to die for
Of the great Division of the North
Only one of those we arranged already
Climbing sierras,
going down looking always for who to fight
I've arrived, and I'm already here
Pancho Villa and his people
With his valiant Gold Sombreros,
They who will die for him
Goodbye Villistas who are there
In Celaya,
Your blood you have given with
Great valor,
Goodbye my beautiful city of Chihuahua,
We won't see you again.
I've arrived, and I'm already here
Pancho Villa and his people
With his valiant dorados
They who will die for him.

The Journal

Dear Sabas,

Just in case you can't find me, I want you to know about things that I am doing. Joaquín Murrieta is still alive. He's still up in the mountains hiding and waiting. The caves told me that the Seven Sisters of the Pleiades guides me, as they did the Painters. It's all there in the paintings if you know how to see it. We will renegotiate the Treaty of Guadalupe Hidalgo. We will return all to the way it was before the conquistadors. Back to the way it was before the horses. Back to the time before the Indians were Indians. Except for us. We can have them. I like horses, so we'll have them. Just a few. We'll have the upper hand for a change. All of us and the Aztecs and maybe the Toltecs. And then I will be able to make pictures of the indigenous people just like Gauguin did. I have a Leica that will make them look real. You think that I am acting crazy, but it's always me and it always will be me. I am collecting the right people to be with me. We need to be together. Now I know not to kill any owls. That is bad luck.

Amor, pesetas, y tiempo para gustarlo,

AKA Pop

Stuck in that same page was a postcard with a picture of Emiliano Zapata and Pancho Villa, both of them sitting on gold, throne-like chairs. Ten other men stood behind them. All of them had their hats off except for one man in front. He was looking away from the camera. Pancho Villa was the only one smiling. They looked like a bunch that might kick your teeth out and take the gold, that unlucky afternoon a long time ago.

22

Everywhere we stopped we asked about him, but no one had seen him. We passed old churches and drove down crowded streets and pushed our way through traffic and clouds of diesel fumes from buses and trucks in village after village, town after town. We took turns driving, one of us sleeping in the back as the other drove. We traveled south on country roads through many villages toward a small town named Chimayo, on the coast, where my grandmother had been born. He'd mentioned it on a card that he sent. There, we got a hotel room for the night.

In the morning, there were just three people in the cafe, along with the old man who was serving and us. He was stoop-shouldered, his hair and beard white, and probably eighty or so years old.

We ordered some coffee and pan dulce, and when we were done and paying I asked the man if he'd lived there for very long.

"All of my life," he said with a smile.

"Do you know of a family here called Beltran?" I said.

"Yes, I knew some Beltrans," he said. "There were two girls and one tall brother who very big in selling chicken shit. They went to the north a long time ago, right after the revolution."

"Are any Beltrans still here?" I said.

"Not that I know of," he said. "A man asked me about the Beltrans last week. He had very blue eyes, like this young man."

"Was it this old man?" I said and showed him the photo.

He took it and looked at it for a long time. "Maybe that's him. Does he wear a green hat, like a soldier's beret?"

"He might."

"I can't say for sure." He squinted his eyes and looked at the photo again. "My eyes are not so good any more. The man with the green hat was an American. He had that in his voice. He gave me five American dollars. And he bought some tamales from a boy who came by, and he gave me one of those, too. He asked me what tribe of Indians the people were here. So I told him that we are mostly Toltecs. The Beltrans had Toltec blood, I know."

"Toltecs?" I said. "That sounds as if that might be him. He's been known to give people tamales, and he wants to know about his family and where they came from."

"Maybe that man was younger," he said. "But, of course, my eyes."

"When was that?" Pete asked.

"Oh, maybe a week ago," he said. He went into the back again, then came out and took some coffee to a couple at another table.

"Maybe he's wearing a different hat," Pete said. "But, like he said, he can't see very well, so it might not have been him."

"Not many people go around in berets down here in the tropics," I said. "Maybe he's doing a Thelonius Monk impression?"

"Maybe so," Pete said. "What's Thelonius Monk?"

"He's that old jazz guy," I said. "He played piano. He liked to wear different kinds of hats. I played a cd of his the other day."

"Oh," Pete said. "What did he like about hats?"

"I don't know," I said. "It was his thing. People gave him hats--homburgs, berets, cowboy hats. He was a classic weirdo, just like your grandfather."

"You're getting kind of crazy, too," he said. "I think you're seeing things."

"Maybe so," I said.

When we got back on the road, I told Pete a story about his great-grandmother. She'd helped my father to be nuts, no doubt about it. Pete knew a little about her, but not much. She'd lived to be ninety-three, so she was still alive when he was five or six, b ut he didn't remember much about her. He had heard some of the stories. I told him about when we went into her house a week after she died. We knew that she had been a nut for expensive clothes and expensive cars, but we were still amazed when we opened the closet doors in her bedroom to find hundreds of dresses and a half-dozen furs, along with hundreds of pairs of shoes and fifty or more hats still in their boxes. Everything looked new, as if it had just been bought. The soles of all of the shoes were clean and without scuff marks. It looked as if she'd never worn them even once out of the house.

"Will you look at all of this crap," my father said. "Jesus, she spent thousands of dollars on all of this stuff."

When she was alive, my father went to her house to see her every couple of days. He'd call her every day to see how she was doing. He was her little, blue-eyed boy. When he was born, my great-grandmother had told my grandmother to put splints on my father's ankle to straighten the ankle on his club foot, but for some unknown reason, she hadn't done it. She had just run from my great-grandfather in Jojutlan to the states instead.

She always wanted new cars, so that she could look and feel like a movie star, so her second husband, Peato, had bought her whatever she wanted. A framed, autographed photograph of Lucille Ball, when she was a starlet, sat on Grandma's vanity, as if she was a relative or a close friend, or as if it was a picture of Grandma herself. Beside it was a photo of herself in a formal dress standing in front of their brand-new pink Buick, her last car before she'd gotten her mist-green Cadillac El Dorado, two years later. In the living room and the dining room crystal chandeliers as big as Volkswagens glistened in the light. In the garage sat the El Dorado with the brushed, stainless steel roof. The car only had nine hundred miles on it, since she'd only gone the quarter mile to church for mass with Peato and, with my father's brother-in-law, to San Francisco and back. And in the closets, there were hundreds of boxes of brand-new shoes and hats that she had bought and never worn except for when she'd tried them on. My father said that the shoe store would bring a dozen or so boxes of new shoes from the shop to her house, so that she could try them all on. She'd buy a pair of green shoes of a certain style, then order red, blue, and yellow shoes, and any other color that was available in that same style. There were hundreds of other dresses that looked as if they had never been worn, so after we'd emptied the closets, it was hard to get into the front room without brushing up against the clothes hanging on racks lined up in the front room and the dining room. Besides that, there were three mink coats, a mink stole, a silver fox coat, and, the real whopper, a coat made from the red fur of an orangutan.

There was a picture that still hung on the living room wall of Marie Antoinette, holding court in an elegant room that looked to be in Versailles, with her ladies in waiting sitting all around her. I had thought, when I was a little kid, that that was my grandmother, and when I stood there that day, then forty years old and looking at all of the clothes and shoes and hats and coats, I figured out that I was right. Marie Antoinette and Lucille Ball were the images that she had of herself, only she wasn't from Paris or Hollywood. She was from Orange County and La Colonia, and before that, a village full of poor people in Jalisco, and when she came to the states she had become, not a movie star, but a strawberry, orange, and tomato picker.

My father and mother were there for two weeks cleaning up the place, with me coming by once in a while. Grandmother's two daughters and son by Peato copiously sorted through the clothes, looking in all of the pockets, searching for any jewelry or money that their nutty mother might have hidden there. The two women were like those old crones who dressed in black in Spain, like vultures pulling on a deer's carcass.

187

Now Grandma's house looked like a department store because of all of the clothes on hangers on the racks. My mother had a bright idea, to sell them to the movie people, so she called a company in Hollywood that dealt in costumes. A woman in a black dress and a black hat right out of the forties showed up. She looked as if she had just stepped out of "Casablanca," as she walked along through the aisles and eyed the dresses, coats, blouses, formal gowns, furs and suits. She looked through the shoes, too, hundreds of boxes of shoes that we had stacked twenty feet long and six feet high along a wall in the living room, below her prints of paintings of Marie Antoinette, who sat in Versaille with her entourage. There were a dozen racks of clothes for her to look through.

"I'll take these furs," she said, "and I'll take these dresses. And all of these shoes, and all of those hats."

"Amazing," my father said. "Someone finally got some use out of all of Mom's stuff. I don't know how any man could've lived with her and let her do all of that buying and buying and buying of everything she saw and everything she wanted."

He didn't seem to consider that he, too, had lived with her for close to twenty years, when she was younger but just as strange. Even then, she had thought of no one but herself, always. I wondered how much the way she was had contributed to making my father nuts. It had certainly made the second husband, Peato, nuts and depressed.

It was almost as if her lifelong dream had come true. Grandma's clothes were going to be in the movies. She wouldn't ever be in the movies, but she had now passed her many things on to famous, or almost famous, movie stars. She had never been rich or famous, but she wanted everything, as if she was the Marie Antoinette of Playa Grande.

23

"Good day. You are called Sabas Catalpa, yes?" he said.

We were in a cafe on the zocalo in Oaxaca, and we were eating chicken. I wiped the grease off of my fingers with a napkin. The man in front of me was tall and thin, and he wore a blue, well-tailored suit.

"Yes, I am," I said. "How do you know me? Are you with the police?" I asked.

"Yes, a certain branch of the police," he said. "We are a federal group but not Federales." He spoke a very formal Spanish.

"Oh," I said, "how did you know who I was?"

"I saw you two when you parked your van," he said. "We have that license number, and it's from California, of course. Have you seen your father? We, too, are looking for him."

"No, not yet. He drove down here from California. He's just on a vacation, you know. We want to contact him, so that we can join him."

"How long did you say he has been here in Mexico?"

"He's been down here for a couple of months."

"Is there any other reason for him to be in Oaxaca?" he said.

"No, just vacation. He's retired, so he has a lot of time."

"Your passports, please," he said.

"No passports, just licenses." I handed him my driver's license and Pete did the same.

"There are many who are against the government in the jungles and the mountains of this area. We must check to see that they are not getting arms from the Americanos," he said.

"Do you have a photo of your father?"

I took out the photo and handed it to him.

"I need to take this photo and give it to my office. They can help you find him." He handed back our licenses, but he kept the photo.

"It's the only photo that we have," I said. "So we need it." I grabbed the photo out of his hand. "We'll just keep looking for him on our own, thanks," I said. His face flushed with anger.

"We are investigating the activities of many foreigners who are in this area," he said. "Our group is less known, but very efficient. There are many who are against the government in Oaxaca and Chiapas."

"Yeah, you said that before. But my father has nothing to do with revolutionaries. He's just a tourist, like us."

"We can find him for you," he said.

"That's okay. We'll find him. He's just a little lost," I said. "He's not a criminal that needs to be hunted down."

"Nevertheless, we will be watching for him," he said. "Since he was in Jalisco he has contacted many suspicious individuals. We can continue to watch for him without the photo. We have our own, so it is not important to get this one. Buenos tardes," he said. He smiled and turned, then walked across the street, into the shade of the trees in the zocalo and across the square. I thought of Efrain's "special group," and I wondered if this was the same bunch.

We got out of town on a road going through another rainforest. I put Monk on the car stereo. The thing with the plainclothes Federale, or whatever he was, was unexpected, and it had shaken me up a little. I needed to soothe my mind, and a little of Monk's clunky music might help me do that. I put it in and turned it on.

I was going fifty through town and then eighty on the highway, even though the signs said the limit was ninety kilometers per hour, about sixty. The trees were a smear of green.

"Take it easy," Pete said. "What's going on?"

190

"That guy might follow us."

"No one's behind us. Take a look."

"I just don't want any part of the Federales. There's no telling what your grandfather's up to."

"We're clear now," he said. We drove through the jungle for a mile or two. Then he said, "What's this music? It's strange."

"It's just different," I said. "This is Monk. Just listen to it and try to figure it out. You don't get it yet, but you will. My father gave this to me. Monk used to wear all kinds of hats, just like your grandfather."

"Grandpa listened to this?"

"No, but he gave us some records, way back."

"He was probably just joking with you," he said.

"No, he wasn't joking," I said.

I'd first heard Thelonius Monk thirty years before, because of my father and because of a beatnik guy named Carlos. He came in and sold my father things once in a while . . . He'd been an honest guy. At least he seemed honest to us. He lived in an old, Spanish-style apartment house down the street from the shop and our house. He always wore a blue watch cap and he had a black goatee with no mustache. My folks talked about him being a beatnik, or a junkie, or both. But my father liked him, whatever he was. Carlos never drove a car or left for a job in the morning. He just hung around the neighborhood and the apartment house all day, every day. He often came into the shop, just to talk, or to tell a joke, or just to say hello. Once in a while, at the end of the month, when Carlos' rent was soon due, he would bring things in to sell to my father. He'd carry in a toaster one day, a bottle of tequila the next, a watch the next month. Some of the stuff might have been hot, but I think Carlos was mostly honest. It looked like stuff that he'd bought, but he obviously wasn't attached to most of the things he brought in to show my father. One afternoon, he came into the shop when I was standing there wiring some carnations for a spray that Pop was making. Carlos had a stack of record albums under his arm

191

and he put them down on the counter.

"Hey, Sabas," he said to my father, who was working on putting together the spray. "Do you think you can help me out today, man? I need some bread for the rent. Maybe you can give me a few bucks for these albums? They're some good ones, man. Fine jazz. I love them, but I need a few bucks right now. You can have them all for twelve bucks. That's only two bucks each."

Pop turned away from his work and looked over at the records from his work table, where he had a casket spray he was working on, white stock and red carnations. Like I said before, a lot of men, and even a lot of women, got casket sprays that were just like that. Simple and clean. He walked over to the counter, picked up the albums, and looked them over. There were some black guys on the covers, a white guy on another, one guy with a goatee just like Carlos', long and black with no mustache.

"They cost me like five bucks each," Carlos said.

"I won't listen to this stuff, Carlos," my father said.

"Get them for your kids, man," he said. "It's like an education. How about ten bucks for all of them?"

My father looked over at me and then back at the albums in his hands.

"Do you want some records?" he said.

I said, "Yes, they look good."

He put the records down on the counter and went to the register and took out a ten dollar bill and handed it to Carlos.

"Here you go, Carlos. What the hell," he said. "Maybe they'll like it."

"Thanks, man," Carlos said. "You know, if I get some bread at a later date, maybe I'll buy these back after you've checked them out for a while. They're excellent jazz, man. Excellent. "

"Sure," my father said, "maybe you can get them back later."

"That's great, man," Carlos said. "Muchas gracias. Ata-watcho," he said. He looked over at me and gave me a nod of recognition, his goatee going up and down, then went out of the

192

shop and back down the street toward his apartment.

"Looks like you guys have some jazz to listen to," my father said. He handed the records to me.

I began to thumb through them. The first album in the stack was by John Coltrane, he and his big sax on the blue and black album cover. On another cover, there was a picture of a black guy with a goatee who sat playing an upright piano in a basement full of junk. He wore a beret and had a machine gun over his shoulder, as if he was in the French Resistance, and his name was Thelonius Monk. Another album was by Miles Davis, a silhouette of someone playing a trumpet that was pointed toward the ground on its cover. Another was Sonny Rollins, who had a long goatee, a saxophone in his hands, and the mouth-piece between his lips, behind him a field of blue. One other was Charlie Mingus, a flamenco dancer on the cover in what looked like Mexico. Dexter Gordon was there, too, along with five or six more in the stack. They were like nothing my brother and I had ever seen before, a strange and exotic bunch of album covers, with photographs of some-strange looking guys I'd never heard of before. The only musicians that I'd heard of at that time were some rhythm and blues guys that my low-rider cousins and half uncle played in their lowered Mercurys and Chevys as they cruised through the towns around the harbor. They played The Penguins and The Del Vikings on their 45 record players. The only jazz that we'd heard was the old jazz, Frank Sinatra or Satchmo, and some Swing music that our parents played once in a while.

I finished putting picks on the carnations and then went up into the house and got Art, and we took the albums upstairs into the attic, where there was an old record player. We put all of the records on the spindle and put the machine on 33 and played the records for a few hours. Foreign sounds came from the instruments, different ways of putting things together. Monk seemed to stagger across the keys of the piano, like a drunken Fred Astaire who was trying to find the right notes. Coltrane's saxophone

193

moaned a long, low mantra. Mingus' band played tunes that sounded as if a party was going on in a Tijuana cantina. Miles Davis hit notes on his trumpet that cried staccato and long and high into each other. Their music just about put us in those smoky rooms that smelled of booze where all of the jazz men hung out.

I let Pete drive for a while, and he drove us through another village with just one tiny store, one Pemex pump out in front of it. Monk still played on the stereo and we rolled south, deep into the jungle, past the ruins that the Mayans had deserted more than a thousand years ago when they'd disappeared into the jungle, for some reason that no one knew or understood, like somebody else I knew.

Down the road we passed more soldiers, but they didn't stop us.

"Tom Batey gave me something to give you," Pete said. "He told me to give it to you at home, when we got there."

"What's that?" I said.

"It's peyote. He said that you'd need it later on."

"Need it? Why?"

"To find Grandpa."

"I've been there already," I said. "It won't tell us where Pop went."

"You know, maybe your father's dead," Pete said. "Maybe he went up into the hills and got killed. Anyway, the Huichole and the Tarahumara use it all the time, right?"

"Pop is alive. He's a tough one to kill. You'd better throw the peyote out the window. If the Federales searched and found it, we'd be in some jail full of rats and cockroaches for a few years. We aren't Huichole or Tarahumara."

24

The narrow road through Chiapas wound along the Guatemalan border. Pete drove while I snoozed a little and watched the green jungle slip by, the shadow of the leaves of the trees and their canopy on the asphalt.

"Isn't Grandpa ever just normal?"

"He has his normal moments. And he had his low times, too. Sometimes he couldn't get off the couch he was so down. He was no hero, that's for sure. But when he was more or less normal he did some interesting things."

We pushed on through Chiapas. Pete kept driving while I looked at my father's journal. It was amazing that he even wrote anything down, he was moving so fast, but here it was. There were entries of where he'd gotten gas, with the dates, the mileage, and the price, which was something he had always done when traveling, for some reason. But the journal showed that he'd stopped in places called Tonal, Tres Picos, Acapetagua, and Puerto Madera, just north of Guatemala. We drove through tunnels formed of the overhanging limbs of trees and through jungle along the two-lane highway. A village would appear with a gas station and a few white houses, a few palapas in front them, a burro standing along the road, short Indians with baskets of coconuts, mangos, papayas, and bunches of bananas to sell.

In one little village, we parked in the shade of a big banyan tree, its roots hanging down from its limbs and growing into the ground. There was no sign saying the name of the village. Maybe it had no name. We went into the store, where an old Indian woman sold us six warm Pacificos and some tortillas, and we went to the cafe down the street under another palapa, where we ordered berria and beans and tortillas from a girl about thirteen or so. An old black dog, its ribs showing like a xylophone, lay in the dirt ten feet away from us, watching us eat, waiting for scraps, no doubt. When we were done and ready to go, Pete threw the dog a couple of tortillas, and I did the same, and the dog gobbled them up.

"Think she has an owner?" Pete said.

"Doubtful," I said. "Looks like she hasn't eaten in a while."

"She just had pups," Pete said. "They ought to feed some of these dogs once in a while."

"They probably have enough trouble feeding themselves," I said.

"What are we doing down here?" Pete said. "It seems like we've been to a hundred villages like this, and we're always too early or too late."

"He sent a card from down here," I said. "He says he's looking for a guy up in the mountains. Some Jesuit priest."

"How are we going to find a guy like that?" Pete said.

"We don't want to find any Jesuit revolutionary," I said. "We might get killed going after him. He's somewhere up in the mountains, and we don't know which mountains. And nobody's going to tell us which mountains."

The girl came to the table and we paid her, and she pushed her black hair out of her face and smiled. I was going to ask her about my father, show her the photograph, but I was tired of that and the man with ojos azules. She smiled again, then went inside.

"We're low on money and energy," I said. "We're almost as bad as that old dog. It's probably time to head north."

"I've been waiting days for that," Pete said. "Maybe we can stop and see that girl at Club Papeete."

"You're dreaming," I said.

"Maybe we can see your Aztec tightrope walker."

"I'd better forget about Aztec tightrope walkers."

"Mom would really get pissed about you screwing some

other woman."

"I think that your mom has almost given up on me."

"Why?"

"I was sick and depressed, and my foot hurt like hell, but she couldn't stand watching me lie on the couch all day. She said that it was probably contagious, and that she couldn't stand it anymore. She didn't want to catch it."

I heard a rumbling sound and a brown Thunderbird sped by, hit one of the big bumps in the road called topes, and flew by us and up the road, north.

25

We got back to Mazatlan in three days, just driving and sleeping in shifts and only stopping for tacos and tortillas at small tiendas and roadside stands along the road north. In Mazatlan, I called Art from a place that had phones you could use for a pocket full of pesos.

"We got a card from Mazatlan two weeks ago," Art said. "He said he's going to go up into the mountains again."

"Why's he going up there this time?"

"He said that's where the real vaqueros are just like they were in the old days."

"So what?"

"I don't know. Maybe he wants to be with cowboys so that he can be a cowboy. He has some friends that he made there, he said, so he's going to go back and see them."

"He's made friends everywhere, but he doesn't have to visit everyone," I said.

"What if you catch up to him and he doesn't want to come home?"

"I guess I'll just have to try to talk him into it," I said. "Can you think of a good reason for him to go home? I'm ready for any suggestions. Look, why don't you stop everything you're doing and come down here and look for him for a while."

"No thanks," he said. "Hey, do you know some woman named Paraquat?"

"Paraquat? You mean Paquette? Cindy Paquette?"

"Yeah, that's it. She called Mom and asked where you are. Then I read in the paper that she shot her ex-husband in the leg and went over and shot at that friend of yours, Brian Martinet, a couple of times. The cops chased her across three counties, but she lost them, so they're still looking for her. They think that she might have gone down into Mexico somewhere."

"Did Mom tell her where I was?"

"She might have, but that was before she went around shooting people. I think Mom told her that you were down in the Sierra de San Francisco, looking for Pop, and that you were heading to Jalisco . . . She's dangerous, I think."

"I knew she was crazy, but I thought she was harmless. I guess she's not harmless after all."

"How could she find you when you're driving all over Mexico?"

"Don't ask me," I said. "But I think that I saw her a couple of times."

"Hell, I know where you are and I couldn't find you," he said. "How could she find you?"

"Maybe it was someone else," I said. "Maybe I'm seeing things?"

"No doubt. It's impossible," he said.

On the ferry from Mazatlan across the Sea of Cortez to La Paz and Pichilinque, I looked at some of the notes that were in his journal again as the ferry ploughed along through wind and waves and stormy weather. He'd written down some Mexican songs, and he'd translated them, for some reason. I looked at the song about Joaquin Murrieta, which I'd seen before and heard sung by an old mariachi in a bar in Baja. So I looked his translation over. There were probably words that changed when the song passed from one mariachi to another. Some lines were crossed out, other lines penciled in. Out the window of the ferry, the gray clouds were reflected in the rough surface of the sea, and I read through his notes and newspaper and magazine clippings, again, and looked at translations of songs, again.

There was one that I'd missed before that he'd written to us but had never gotten around to mailing, just like a lot of other letters in the journal.

The Journal

Dear Familia,

I was thinking about all of the gringos that I have known, about all of my gringo friends, and I figured out that they didn't do anything wrong. They didn't take California and the rest of the Southwest away from Mexico. That happened way back when everybody was pouring into California to look for gold and when everybody was going to Texas to get a hacienda and hang out at the Alamo. I thought, What in the hell was I thinking when I wanted to take California and the rest back for Mexico? The Mexican government would probably screw things up just as bad as the Americans have. It would take them a long time to learn how to do it all. And there is already plenty of good Mexican food, so they don't need any more of that in the Southwest, even though there is a lot of bad food that they try to say is Mexican food. And a lot of places are just fine the way they are.

Then I thought about taking Mexico and the whole Southwest back for the Indians. Even though there are still a few people who aren't part Indian in Mexico, after all of these years since Cortez landed, there is one hell of a lot of people that are part Indian, me included. All anyone has to do is look in a mirror to know that he's part Indian. And if you've ever been to a reservation, you know about the old and rusty cars that sit around waiting to be fixed or junked, or both. And then there are the beer cans along the side of the road that someone threw out the window going ninety. They treat everything like it goes away sooner or later, but those cans and plastic bags and styrofoam cups never go away. So taking it all back for the Indians would be a mess. How much would the part-Indian people get? Would they get more if they are half Indian than someone who is a sixteenth Indian, say? Would those who are a sixteenth Indian get one sixteenth as much as someone who was all Indian? Besides that, how could anyone prove how much Indian they are, since their gene pool is so stirred up that no one knows who's what anymore?

I thought about what would happen to the Grand Canyon and Hollywood and Disneyland and Yosemite. What would happen to Big Sur and the Redwoods and the Giant Sequoias, and The Caverns in New Mexico, if Mexico or the Indians had those places? Everyone there would have to learn Spanish or Apache, or some other Indian language, maybe, and that would take a very long time, and even after years the gringos still wouldn't know how to pronounce Puerto Vallarta right. What would happen to all of the jazz singers if they had to learn Spanish or Indian?

An old woman in Jojutlan told me that my grandfather had kept twenty thousand gold pesos and a lot of horses for me. But that all happened a long time ago, and everything that was said by my grandfather then is a long time forgotten now. He probably buried those gold pesos and forgot to tell anyone where they were. The family there knows that I should have gotten something, of course, but they positively don't know what. No one had any plans to cheat anyone else out of anything. Whatever I was supposed to get has disappeared with the old people, my grandfather and his brothers and sisters. Efrain and his wife Elena, and the rest of the family there now, are a good bunch of people, who should just be left alone to look out the window at the lake and live peacefully in that quiet village of Jojutlan. So that's what I'm going to do, leave them all alone. All I need is one horse, and I can afford to buy that, and all I need is one bed to sleep in. And all I want to eat is two eggs in the morning, like Steinbeck said, along with a couple cups of coffee.

The Joaquin and the Gauguin in me likes what I'm going to do. So I have called off my revolution and decided to go up into the mountains and become a vaquero, for a while, with those few vaqueros who are left. If I decide to change my mind and take it all back, Mexico included, then I'll take it back for the animals, the eagles and the hawks, the cougars and the bears and the buffalo, since they were the ones who had it

202

all in the first place, and they deserve a break, after all of these years that the men have had it and have made a mess of it. Besides that, I owe it to the owls, since I shot them that time, for no good reason, and I'd like to be long rid of that bad luck that shooting them brought me.

Someone tell me, who is the Cisco Kid?

Amor, pesetas, y tiempo para gustarlo,

Sabas Joaquín Gauguín,

Your Pop

203

26

We got off the ferry in Pichilinque. Outside of La Paz stood the burnt remains of the orange and blue circus tent that we'd gone to in Mulege a few weeks earlier. There was only the roof, standing like a big umbrella in a field on the main road. I pulled the van over and stopped for gas across from the circus. The tent's poles and ropes and lines still stood, but there were big holes in the cloth on the sides, so you could see inside. While the attendant filled the tank with gas, I got out and looked across the street. The Aztec princess and the knife thrower came out of a trailer and went into the burned out tent. I was still convinced that that had been her, in La Paz, but whoever it was, she was just as beautiful as this woman. They were in their costumes and it looked as if they were ready for the show. A few people stood talking near the booth where they had sold tickets, and some others stood looking through the holes of the half-burnt tent. Pete got out of the truck and stood beside me.

"That tent is history," Pete said.

We drove across the road, pulled up next to the tent's remains, and got out of the van. Through the bleachers, I could see the knife thrower and the Indian woman standing inside. They were talking and looking at the damage. A man in a straw cowboy hat just like a few million others in Mexico stood next to me, and I asked him what had happened.

"The fire was last night," he said. "They don't know how it started. Maybe someone did it."

"Why would anyone want to burn a circus?" I said.

He shrugged. "Some people. You understand?" He touched his head.

"Was anyone hurt?" I said.

"I don't think so," he said. "That old woman there saw

some-body out here, after the show."

"Who put it out?"

"The knife thrower saved the animals, and the bomberos used their hose on the tent."

"Was he there when it started?"

"He was feeding the animals, he said. He saved the puma and the horses."

Under the square roof of the tent, the four bleachers still stood, like the skeletons of elephants, circling the center ring.

"They're going to have the show anyway," the man said. "The old hombre will not give up because of a little fire, he said. You see, they're selling tickets."

A dozen people stood in a line near the ticket booth.

"We have to see this," I told Pete. "These people are an endangered species."

We bought two tickets and walked inside what remained of the tent and sat down, up in the bleachers. The clowns, the knife thrower and the beautiful Aztec woman, the tattooed man with his chairs, and finally the Aztec woman, once again with her feathers flying as she walked the tightrope barefooted. All of them did their parts as if nothing had happened to their tent. For the final act, the Toltec midgets came out and did their pyramid trick, as before, only now I had seen it twice before, once in Mulege and once in Oaxaca when Tom had spiked the pulque.

Afterwards, we walked back into the trailers. The Aztec woman was speaking to the knife thrower, and when we came up, she glanced at us and smiled, and then she got into a pickup truck and drove away south, toward La Paz. She was lovely and beautiful and the whole deal. And I wanted to follow her but I couldn't. Maybe later, I thought. Maybe I'd run into her again, somehow, in my dreams.

I went up to the knife thrower.

"Pardonome," I said, "does that Indian woman in your act have a twin sister, or a sister who looks a lot like her, who lives in La Paz?"

"No, I think that she has no sisters," he said. "But she is from La Paz."

"Does she sometimes work in La Paz, in a place called Club Papeete?"

"No," he said. "She just works with me and then she walks the wire."

"I thought I saw her in La Paz."

"La Paz is a long drive from here. There are a lot of beautiful Indian women in Mexico, señor. You must be mistaken." He excused himself and then walked to his trailer and went inside.

"I told you that you were dreaming," Pete said. "Let's get going. I need some food."

"First let's go and see Don Diego again."

"He didn't seem to help much last time we saw him," he said.

"Sure he did. He gave us encouragement, which is a big help. Who cares if anyone can do 'The I Ching.' Like he said, he's better at it than most people, just because he's old and he's done it thousands of times. Besides that, I think he's a good guy, and I like him. I like to support the good people I meet. I like the old guy, and it's a lot of fun, don't you think?"

"Yeah, it makes you think, I guess," Pete said.

So we walked over to the old trailer where Don Diego had been before. The sign that was painted on the side of the trailer had changed a little.

Now it read:

**don Francisco, el Indio
Con Tres Cientos Años
Memorias del Futuro**

"Is this the same guy?" I said. "Wasn't his name Don Diego before?"

"Yeah, I think so," Pete said.

"I guess he got a little older, too," I said. "Last time he was

206

only two hundred years old."

We went inside, and it was dark, as before. The old man was still sitting in his chair, sleeping or meditating, or both. I smelled sage and tequila and pipe tobacco. This was the same place all right. Don Diego, who apparently was now Don Francisco, sat in the blue light, with the pile of the long sticks and his dog-eared copy of "The I Ching" on the table in front of him, along with half a bottle of tequila and a short glass with half an inch of tequila in it.

He opened his eyes and smiled. "Good afternoon, once again, caballeros," he said, looking up at us as he poured an inch of tequila into his glass. "It's good to see you. So did you find what you wanted?"

"No, not yet," I said. "Didn't your name used to be Don Diego?"

"Yes, it was, but I got bored being Don Diego, so I changed it, so that I could see how it is to be someone else for a while."

"And didn't you used to be two hundred years old?" Pete said.

"That's just advertising, trying to get more people to visit my trailer," he said. "Anyway, there are so many two-hundred-year-old Indians these days." He raised his glass. "To the gods who protect us," he said and took a sip of his tequila. "Do you have more questions for me?"

"I have a lot of questions," I said.

"Perfecto," Don Francisco said.

Pete and I sat down, and Don Francisco picked up the sticks once more and then passed them from hand to hand, putting some down to his right, then his left, marking a solid line or a broken line on a piece of paper in front of him, until there were six lines, some solid, some broken, once again. Finished, he reached over and grabbed the bottle of tequila and poured himself another drink.

"Fine," he said. "Which trigrams do we have today?" He

put the book off to his right and grabbed the sticks again. "There's an easier way of doing this, but using the sticks is the best. It gives you more time to dwell on your question."

Like before, he'd drawn the six lines in the notebook that sat on the table in front of him.

"How's Columbo doing?" I asked.

"Columbo?" he said.

"He's a cop," I said.

"Okay . . . So 'The Traveler' with a couple of moving lines. 'Success in small matters. Persistence with regard to traveling brings good fortune. Fire upon a mountain. The superior man employs wise caution in administering punishments and does not suffer the case brought before him to be delayed. For the bottom place. Trifling with unimportant matters the traveler draws upon himself. Calamity.'

"For the second place. 'The traveler reaches an inn with his valuables still nestling safely in the bosom of his robe. He gains the loyalty of a young servant. There will be no trouble.'

"Line three: 'Owing to the traveler's lack of caution the inn is burnt down to the ground and he no longer enjoys the young servant's loyalty. Persistence now would lead to trouble . . . Traveling on a downward path, our sense of duty and fitness is impaired . . . '

"Line four: 'The traveler reaches a place where he obtains the money needed for his expenses, yet laments that there is no joy in his heart. His wandering to that place is indicated by the unsuitable position of this line. His obtaining money for expenses brings him no joy . . . '

"The fifth place: 'While pheasant shooting, he loses an arrow. In the end he wins praise and attains to office. Both of these are bestowed from above.'

"The sixth: 'A bird manages to burn its own nest. At first the traveler laughs, but then has cause to shout and weep. A cow is lost through carelessness--misfortune! . . . The loss of a cow through carelessness means that no news will ever be obtained of something we have lost or are about to lose.'"

"Is that all?" I said.

"A bit more. A moving line at the top, and that hexagram is . . . 'The Small Get By . . . Success. Persistence in a righteous course brings reward. Small things can be accomplished now, but not great ones. When birds fly high, their singing is out of tune. The humble, but not the mighty, are favored now with great good fortune.' And for the top changing line, 'Instead of accosting him, he passed him by. The bird flew away from him-- misfortune in the form of natural calamity and deliberate injury.' You are being arrogant, and you should avoid doing that.

The Traveler

—————————
——— ———
—————————
—————————
——— ———
——— ———

The Small Get By

——— ———
——— ———
—————————
—————————
——— ———
——— ———

"And that's all there is today," he said. "I hope that you've answered the questions you asked."

"Yes, I guess so," I said. "I'll have to think about it."

"These are just recommendations," he said, "that might help you look at what is there but is not at first apparent. Reflect on what I read to you. Of course, what will happen in the future is anyone's guess. You can use this in approaching whatever happens."

"I like it, even though I don't really know if I believe in it," I said. "But thanks."

"You're welcome." He held out his hand. "That will be a hundred pesos."

"Wasn't it seventy pesos last time?" I said.

"As you notice, some things change," he said and smiled.

I put a hundred peso bill in his palm. Then he lit his pipe and held out the piece of paper where he had drawn the two sets of lines, and I took it. The smoke billowed from his pipe and filled the trailer so that we were all inside of a blue cloud again.

"Where are you from?" I said.

"I told you before, all over," he said. Then he leaned back in his chair and closed his eyes. It looked as if he went to sleep.

"Do you know the alambrista, that Indian woman?"

"She's my great-, great-, great-, great-granddaughter."

"Does she ever go down to work in La Paz?"

"When she can."

"In a strip club?"

"You must be mistaken."

"I saw her down there."

"I don't think so, but if you saw someone as beautiful as she is, think of it as good luck."

"I can't get her out of my thoughts," I said.

"You'll be all right," he said. "It will probably pass, like everything else."

"Maybe so," I said, "but I doubt it."

"That's also possible," he said. "Bad luck, like killing an owl."

"Yes," I said, "that is bad luck, too, isn't it."

We got up and walked outside, and Pete said, "Maybe he really has memories of the future."

"Maybe so," I said. "A three-hundred-year-old Indian must know something."

"What did you ask this time?" Pete said.

"I didn't ask anything," I said.

"How is that supposed to work?" Pete said.

"Now I can make up questions as we go along."

"Maybe so," he said. "I don't know about that stuff."

"There's nothing to know, really."

"I wonder if I'll ever believe in anything," he said.

"That's up to you. It's more difficult to make up your own rules, I think. Without them you're running around like your grandfather, going nowhere fast."

"That's too bad," he said.

"Yes, it is too bad," I said.

27

Back in San Ignacio, the next afternoon, we went to the Rice and Beans Motel, got a room and cleaned up, and then went to their restaurant to eat. The old man we'd met before, Don Ramon, was still sitting at the same table, reading his Bible, its pages and leather cover curled and dog eared. He held his right hand up when he saw us, as if he was a crossing guard stopping traffic.

"It's very strange about your father," he said. "Raul told me that he rode off into the canyons, and they looked for him, but could not find him."

"When was this?" I said.

"A week ago," he said. "One night he rode off on Raul's mule, and he never came back."

"Then he's still up there somewhere," I said.

"As I said, there's buried treasure up there," he said, "put there by someone--Indians, or conquistadors, or priests, or deserters."

"Yes," I said, "you told me about that before. Everyone told me about it. But why would anyone bury anything worth anything way the hell up there, in the middle of nowhere, where they couldn't get it if they wanted to?"

"This is very mysterious," he said. "The Painters could fly, they say, so maybe they just flew up there. Anyway, they say that they were here three thousand years ago, and that they left gold and silver behind."

"Where do you think they went?"

"They have been gone for so long that no one knows the time," he said. "A few Pai Pai are in the mountains in the north,

212

some Sari on islands near Guaymas." Don Ramon took his hat off and set it on the table. "Anyway, your father is somewhere up there."

"Who knows? Maybe he'll find something," I said.

"Maybe so," Don Ramon said. "There are probably many good things that are buried on the beach in Hollywood."

"Hollywood isn't on the beach, Don Ramon," I said.

"Of course it is," he said. "I saw it on the television. You know your novia friend came here asking about you. Did she ever find you?"

"Did she drive an old brown Thunderbird with dirty windows?" I asked. "Yes, she did find me."

We sat around the fire that next night in the canyon with Raul and Carlos, who had taken us once again into the canyons that morning. The clicking of the rocks hitting each other echoed around us from something or someone coming through the canyon. I thought of the mountain lion, and then of Cindy, but when I turned, there was a man in what seemed to be the traditional white straw cowboy hat and with white clothes running past us through the dry part of the river bed.

"Esteban!" Raul said into the darkness. "Stop and have a drink."

A man carrying a backpack and wearing a straw cowboy hat circled back into the light and came to stand by the fire. He stood close to the fire and warmed his hands, the firelight on his dark face. Carlos got a tin cup and poured some tequila in it, then handed it to him.

"How are you, amigo?" Raul said.

Esteban took off his hat and held it at his side. "Muy buen, gracias," he said.

"Where are you coming from?" I asked him.

"San Ignacio. I was there all day. Now I'm going home."

"That's a long walk," I said. "How much further is your

house?"

"Only ten kilometers, or so." He sipped the tequila and watched the fire. He set the cup of tequila down on the ground. Then he took his small pack off of his shoulder and opened it and took out a plastic bottle of water and took a drink.

"You walked all of the way from San Ignacio today?" I said.

"Yes, I walk there and back every two weeks," he said. "I am a very good walker."

"Maybe you saw an old man on my mule in the canyon today?" Raul said.

"An old man came to my house a week ago. He bought some cheese and beans and tortillas from me. He was going to the Canyon de Guadalupe."

"Good," Raul said, "now we know which way to go."

"How far is that?" I asked.

"Not far," Raul said. "A day's ride."

"Muchas gracias for the tequila," Esteban said and smiled. "Now I go home."

"Travel safely," Raul said.

Esteban handed Raul the tin cup and turned and jogged off through the rocks. The clicking sound of the river rocks that he ran through echoed in the canyon.

"How does he walk through all of these rocks at night without tripping?"

"He knows where every rock is, even in the dark."

"Maybe it's like my father always said, 'Watch where you're going, or you'll trip.'"

"Esteban can walk to town any time he wants to, night or day, and he doesn't have to feed a mule."

When I got into the tent and lay there for fifteen minutes or so, I heard the growling, hissing sound of the mountain lion again.

"Who's he calling now, Raul?" I said, loud enough for him to hear me in their tent.

"He's calling your father," Raul said. "Who else?"

We drank our camp coffee the next morning, and Raul went off to take a leak, and when he came back he said, "I saw that mountain lion's tracks back there again. They look fresh, from last night."

"That must be the same one from before," I said.

"Probably so," Raul said. "Who can tell? I think that he's hungry and he's following the mules and the burros."

"Maybe he's following us," I said.

"Maybe so," Raul said. "He eats everything that he catches."

An hour or so down the trail we crossed the stream, and Raul pointed out Esteban's stone house up on the rim. From there we rode through another canyon with a dry creek bed. Raul saw more lion tracks all along the trail.

"I should have my rifle," he said, "just in case."

"That would be good," I said. "How much further?"

"Just three or four hours more," Raul said. "We'll be there before dark."

"Maybe he's found some of that gold and he's already gone, " Pete said.

Raul laughed. "He knows that you're after him, and he doesn't want you to find him."

"We just want to keep him out of jail and out of the mental hospital," Pete said. "We just want him to come home without getting himself killed."

"Where is home?" Raul said.

"Up north, in California, of course," Pete said.

"Perhaps it is," Raul said. "Maybe for him going home is like going to jail."

"Maybe so," I said.

The deeper into a finger of the canyons we rode, and the deeper we got, the more dark my mind felt, just as it had

215

before. I didn't know how far I could stand following Pop any longer to the place where he was.

We looked for him in many canyons for five days, with no luck, so we rode the mules back to the village of San Francisco de La Sierra. The canyons were a maze we had escaped from. The figures on the walls of the canyon had been watching those who passed for three or four thousand years.

When we rode up to Raul's house, I saw that my father's car was still there. Then I saw a mule tied up under a tree. The mule had no saddle on its back. At the tree, we dismounted and tied the mules and donkeys there, and Raul and Carlos started to take the saddles off.

My father walked out from the cabin next to Raul's house and smiled at us and waved. He wore his black Stetson back off of his forehead.

"Hey, strangers. How's your como estamos?" he said.

Raul's wife came out of her house and went to Raul and hugged him.

"Glad to see you," Pop said.

"'Glad to see you'?" I said. "We've been trying to catch up to you for a month."

"So I heard," he said. "What's the problem? Is something wrong?"

"No, you just need to come back home. You need to see a doctor. Get some kind of medicine. It will help you feel better, I think."

"Hell, I feel perfect," he said.

High above him, a red-tailed hawk circled, higher and higher, until it was just a red glimmer in the sky.

"I'm fine." His face had that youthful glow that he got sometimes. "And I'm positively not going to take any damn medicine."

"You need to go home, even if you don't take any medicine. Mom's worried about you. She thinks you're going to end up dead down here. And I think she's right."

216

"I'm going to end up dead somewhere, no matter what," he said.

"This revolution stuff is going to get you into a lot of trouble," I said.

"That was before. Hell, I'm not making any trouble," he said. "I'm just trying to fix things up."

"What things?"

"The whole mess. I've got it all just about figured out."

"How's that?"

"It's complicated. It would take me a few days to tell you about it."

"What about the shop?"

"What about it?"

"It's closed now. You can open it again."

"Why would I want to do that?" he asked. "I've just gotten rid of it. Screw the shop."

"You need it to make money."

"I've got enough money for now."

"So you won't come with us?"

"I'm leaving and you're leaving, and I'm going my way, alone. Unless you want to come with me."

"Where in the hell are you going now?"

"First Hermosillo, to look up some of Murrieta's relatives. Then Chihuahua and the Copper Canyon. I'm going to live with the Tarahumara."

"That's a little loco, Pop. What do they have that you need?"

"They can run like antelope, forever," he said. "Besides that, they never signed a treaty with Mexico or anyone else. Just my kind of people. I can't run, but maybe they can teach me how to fly," he said. "Hell, come with me, both of you."

"We can't come with you," I said. "That's wild country out there."

"Why not try it? We'd have a good time."

"I've got to get back, Grandpa," Pete said. "I have a girl

waiting for me, or anyway, I used to. Besides, I like it up there."

"As you wish," he said. "Maybe you can come and see me later, whatever the case." He gave me a hug, and then he hugged Pete.

"Just remember that in a hundred years or less, you won't know the difference. I wish you both love, money, and time to enjoy it," he said.

Then he got in his Dodge and headed down the dirt road toward the highway, making a huge plume of dust so that his car disappeared like a star does when the sun rises.

28

Three days later, we were back in Playa Grande, looking at the waves as I drove up to my old house, where Jean now lived alone. I parked, and we went to the door. It was almost midnight. We knocked, and Jean came to the door and let us in.

"Did you find him?" she said.

"Almost," I said.

"I thought you were supposed to bring him back."

"He wouldn't come back with us," I said.

"Why not? You were supposed to make him come back."

"It was impossible to turn him around," I said.

"Then it was a waste of time," she said.

"No, it was actually a good trip," I said. "You look good. Why so happy?"

"It's good to see my son come home safe and healthy, and I guess it's good to see you, too . . . Would you two like a couple of beers?"

"Sure," I said.

We went into the kitchen and sat down at the table, and she got us each a bottle of Mexican beer.

"Thanks."

"That old cheerleader friend of yours, Cindy Paquette, went on a rampage. She was front-page news."

"What did she do?"

"She shot her husband's house up, then she went down to Laguna and took a couple of potshots at that friend of yours, Brian Martinet. Lucky for him she ran out of bullets and threw the gun at him. Then she took off and disappeared for a while, somewhere. But now I read that she's in the hospital, down in

Fairview. Did she know that you were down in Mexico?"

"I told her that I was heading there," I said, "but nothing specific."

"I know. Your mom. She probably talked to her. Your mom knew where you were, didn't she?"

"Art probably told her. He knew where we were most of the time."

"Brian gave the gun to the cops, and then the cops showed up here."

"Why?"

"They asked about your gun, the one your grandfather gave your father. They'd registered it downtown a couple of years ago, when your dad stole that lock that time. They knew you had it before she did, whatever the case."

"It was stolen just before we went after Pop. There was a half of a peanut butter sandwich and an empty glass of milk sitting in the kitchen, and the gun was gone. I didn't even call the cops, since I was in a hurry and I knew they couldn't do anything anyway."

"Well, you have to go downtown and talk to them," she said. "They think you gave it to her."

"Sure," I said. "I always give people my gun so that they can shoot people."

"She got it somewhere." She pushed her hair out of her face.

"She ripped it off from my place, then she tried to shoot people," I said. "That's what happened. Besides that, the cops can have that gun. It's bad luck, like killing owls."

I dropped off Pete and headed back to the apartment. When I got there, I saw that there was a bullet hole in my front door, chest high. I had an idea who might have done that. Inside, the bullet had put a hole right through the sailboat in my Winslow Homer print. The bullet had gone right through the sail of the boat and into the wall. At least it hadn't gone into me

220

this time.

Fairview County Hospital was three mint green monoliths in the middle of a forest of glass buildings. The visiting hours for the mental facility were from 5:00 p. m. to 8:00 p. m., so I got there at six. There was a large room with three couches and eight easy chairs with a view of the Pacific. It was a nice place to visit, but the company was questionable. Cindy Paquette sat across from me and wiggled her right leg as she looked out the window, then back at me. They had her on something, probably Thorazine, and she had a stare that made her eyes seem as deep as Lake Tahoe. Her hair was cut short, and it lay flat on her head, as if it hadn't been washed in a couple of weeks.

"How are you doing, Cindy?" I asked.

She just looked at me.

"The nurse said that your kids visited you yesterday."

"They came and talked to me but they talked for a minute," she said. "I think that they came yesterday."

"Look, Cindy, I'm sorry about not giving you Brian's number, but he couldn't talk to you. His wife's jealous, I think."

"In just a little while the doctor said that I can go and see my girls."

"I got you this azalea plant," I said. "I thought that you might like it."

"I can have flowers," she said. "I don't know what else I can have, but I can have flowers. They're very pretty and red."

"Sure," I said. "You know, I thought that I saw you down in Mexico when I was there. Did you go down into Mexico?"

"I have a lot of money that they don't know about, you know. Mexico? I think so. I can go a lot of places in my car."

"I'm sorry that I couldn't help you out with your kids. But now you'll be able to see them more, when you get better."

"I'm going to see them real soon, the doctor said."

"Sure you will," I said. "How did you go way down into Mexico all alone?" I said. "It's a long ways."

"A nice man helped me drive. Chencho. He was a good

221

driver. He's from Guatemala, he said. I don't know."

"Were you way down in Oaxaca with this Chencho?"

"We were some place, in some mountains, for a while. Your mother said that you were there, so I went there, I think, so that you could help me."

"Did you have a gun with you?"

"I got a gun but I threw it away someplace."

"Did you know that I had a gun?"

"You're a policeman," she said. "All policemen have guns."

"I was a policeman," I said. "But not anymore."

"It was an old cowboy gun. It stopped shooting, so I threw it away."

"Well that's good, I guess," I said.

"Chencho had another gun anyway," she said.

"Oh, that's not good," I said. "Did you have anything to do with a fire down in Baja? A circus?

"Chencho made me make the fire," she said. "I don't like fire, but Chencho does, and he told me that he would help me to get my kids if I helped him, so I helped him make the fire, but I like the circus, and he's just mad at his Indian wife."

"His Indian wife?"

"He said that he has an Indian wife in the circus, who walks on a wire, and she has his kids and he wants them, and he wants her, but she doesn't come back, so he wants to stop the circus and then she'll come back, he said."

"Did he start the fire at the circus?"

"I'm not supposed to tell anyone, but I saw him with the gasoline, and I helped him, and when the fire started to go he ran out and we left really fast."

"You'd better be quiet about that fire or you'll never get out of here, Cindy."

"Yes, I'll be quiet, like I'm supposed to be," she said.

"Where did this Chencho guy go?" I said.

"He just went somewhere."

"In Mexico?"

"I think so. Down in Mexico." She fidgeted with her fingers and she was very spaced out, so who knows what was true.

"There's a bullet hole in my door, Cindy. Did you shoot at my door?"

"Maybe, but I can't remember a lot of things."

"Okay, you take it easy, Cindy. Get better, so that you can be with your kids."

"Okay, I'll stay here and be good and then my kids will come and we'll play in the yard," she said. "I really hope that I can."

"I hope so, too," I said.

29

Six months passed just as fast as six running horses. I was in California proper, spending a few months there after a staying a couple of months in Cinco Casas. We'd closed the shop for good. My father said he didn't want it anymore and he wasn't going to work there anymore. I had no taste for running it. No one else was up to it, either. I figured my father might come back, when he finally descended a few thousand feet, but I didn't know when.

When we'd gotten back, I'd called Efrain, down in Jojutlan, to tell him where we'd found Pop, that we'd found him and then he just took off again.

"Maybe he'll return to Jojutlan," he said. "He likes it here, I know . . . But listen to something very interesting. Berta sold the old casa in town that she got when she got married. It was where our great-grandfather lived before he died. On the first day that this man owned the house, he went in with a metal detector. And he looked all around and guess what he found? Twenty thousand gold pesos were plastered up in a wall in the old house."

"Where did that come from?"

"Our great-grandfather, probably. It was probably there to hide it from the Villistas. Nobody else had gold pesos. He was probably saving it for someone, but he forgot about it and never told anyone, and then he died. Now that bastardo with the metal detector has it all."

Three more months passed and I got a letter from Pop that he'd sent to me at Jean's place. We hadn't heard anything from him since we'd seen him in the Sierra, so I was hopeful that he was settling down, ready to come home, perhaps.

Dear Sabas,

I've been here with the Tarahumara for more than six months now, up here in the mountains. My friend Don Tomas can run fast enough to catch a deer. I think that like the Painters they can also fly. There's no electricity and very few cars up here, so it's almost like the old days. An old man who is two hundred years old is teaching me about the plants, the animals, and the stars. I am starting to see this world.

Someday I may go back home, to California, but I can't say when. It took a long time for me to find this place. And Joaquin and Gauguin are still with me, like old friends.

The Tarahumara move from place to place, and I travel with them and go where they go, so I can't tell you where I'll be. But I am here and if you come perhaps you will find me.

Amor, pesetas, y tiempo para gustarlo,

Sabas Joaquin Gauguin,

Your Pop

I called Pete to see if he wanted to go down and find him.

"I can't go this time," he said. "I can't chase Grandpa around all of the time. I've got school and a new girlfriend that I think I love. If you find him, maybe I'll go down there and see you later."

"That's too bad," I said. "I'd like your company."

Then I went to my mother's turquoise bungalow.

I told her that Pop had sent me a letter. It was the first time he'd written in close to a year.

"He'll come down one of these days," she said. "Take some lithium with you."

"What am I supposed to do with that?"

"Maybe you can put some in his ice cream," she said, tears in her eyes.

"I doubt they have ice cream where he is," I said.

But she went into her bedroom and came out with the blue plastic container of pills and handed it to me.

"Try to get him to come back this time," she said. "Tell him that I miss him. We all miss him."

"I will," I said. But I doubted that he would ever come back.

She stood in the doorway behind the screen and waved goodbye as I drove away.

I stopped at the house to see Jean. She didn't completely hate me, it seemed, so she gave me a kiss even though she probably thought I was like a wild animal standing at her door.

"You aren't taking Pete with you, are you?" she said.

"No, he can't go," I said. "He's got school, he says."

"That's good," she said. "I don't want him to get lost in Mexico, with the rest of the Catalpas."

Back at my apartment I packed up the van, then locked the apartment up as best I could. I didn't want any more visitors. In Chihuahua, I'd be searching blind again, since he'd given no specifics. But maybe this time I could join him for a while. Maybe he'd stay still long enough for that. He was out in the wild country with the mountain lions. I drove through the Mojave Desert and toward the Copper Canyon and the Tarahumara. The odds were against my catching up to him.

Around midnight, I stopped for gas at a station just off the highway. There was a cafe with a red neon sign that said Good Home Cooking down the street, and I parked in back of it and got out of the car. In the parking lot behind the cafe, it was dark enough to see the stars thick in the desert sky. I stood there for a while and made a constellation of a horse out of six of the brightest stars. Then I went in and got a cup of coffee and some

226

pie. When I finished, I came out into the parking lot again, and I looked up. The horse had disappeared into the billions of stars around it. I got in the van and drove southeast, Dexter Gordon playing his sax, as I headed into Mexico.

17611750R00121

Made in the USA
Charleston, SC
19 February 2013